WINDS OF CHANGE

When Kate returns to Stony Ridge Farm, she doesn't expect to find a strange man living in her cottage. Who is Grant and why is he there? Her parents trust him, but a mysterious visitor arouses Kate's suspicions. What has happened to divide the farming community and cause conflict between friends? She determines to discover the truth. As secrets from the past cause turmoil in the present, Kate finds herself questioning her own feelings . . .

FAY WENTWORTH

WINDS OF CHANGE

Complete and Unabridged

LINFORD
Leicester

First published in Great Britain in 2009

First Linford Edition
published 2010

British Library CIP Data

Wentworth, Fay.
    Winds of change. - -
    (Linford romance library)
    1. Country life- -Fiction. 2. Strangers- -Fiction.
    3. Love stories.
    4. Large type books.
    I. Title II. Series
    823.9′2–dc22

    ISBN 978–1–44480–493–5

Published by
F. A. Thorpe (Publishing)
Anstey, Leicestershire

Set by Words & Graphics Ltd.
Anstey, Leicestershire
Printed and bound in Great Britain by
T. J. International Ltd., Padstow, Cornwall

1

'Hi, Mum, it's me, Kate. I'm ringing to let you know I'm coming home. Don't worry about Holly Cottage; I'll clean it up when I get there. Just put the kettle on!'

Kate Bramwell hung up, smiling. She was never sure how to finish an answerphone message. Her mobile beeped; she had forgotten to charge the battery! Oh, well, she smiled in anticipation, she would soon be home.

She sat back in the front seat of her camper van and started the engine. As she tucked her thick chestnut hair behind her ears, her green eyes sparkled. The roads were quiet and her thoughts drifted back to the campsite in Portugal that had been her base for the last few weeks.

It had been fun; students from all walks of life and from different countries — she had learned a lot and the social life had been great . . . Her eyes misted over; too great maybe, hence the sudden homesickness for Stony Ridge Farm and the dash across the water to England.

Now, she was almost there. All being well, she would arrive in Larchpool by evening.

In her mind's eye she could see the farm, stone built and sturdy, cocooned by the mellow border hills climbing smoothly, in the distance the craggier rocks of the Welsh mountains. It had been almost twelve months and she could count on the fact that nothing would have changed.

Perhaps now she could settle for a while, take a job, use the knowledge she had gained at Business College. And what of the friends she had left behind? She had kept in touch, but their lives had moved on too and she had been so busy enjoying herself . . .

Her thoughts turned to her young sister, Rosa. She would be sixteen now.

Would she have changed? Kate felt a sudden stab of yearning as she put her foot down on the accelerator.

At Stony Ridge Farm, Evie unloaded the shopping onto the kitchen table and made coffee. Taking a sip, she heaved a sigh of relief and pressed the flashing answer-phone. She frowned as she heard her daughter's message. Picking up the phone she re-dialled the number and waited impatiently as the metallic voice instructed her to leave a message.

'Kate? Lovely to hear you're coming home at last. Ring me back, please. There's a small problem,' she hesitated, 'ring me soon.'

She hung up, feeling the inadequacy of her message. She must talk to Kate before she arrived. So much had changed!

She stood staring at the profusion of carrier bags, her thoughts with her daughter. Kate had always been impulsive and Evie had been quietly worried as the weeks had turned into months and Kate and her camper van had lurched from one country to another. The last postcard they had received had been from Portugal where Kate had taken a job in a restaurant. Had she phoned from there? Or was she back in this country?

Evie shrugged and began to unpack the groceries.

'Any chance of a cuppa?' Her husband's voice interrupted her thoughts and she jumped.

'Owen! I didn't hear you come in.' Evie refilled the kettle as he shook off his boots.

'My, but it's warm out there for April.' He mopped his brow as he sank into a chair. 'I hope it's not going to be another dry summer. Bad for the crops.'

'Good for business though.' Evie smiled as Owen grunted. 'You'll get used to the changes, Owen.'

Evie patted him on the shoulder as she put the steaming mug in front of him, but her glance was concerned.

Settling herself opposite she pushed the shopping to one side.

'We've had a message from Kate.'

'Oh?' Owen brightened. 'What did she say?'

'She's coming home.'

'Really?' He grinned. 'That's great. When?'

Evie shrugged. 'That's the trouble, she didn't say. And she offered to clean up Holly Cottage when she gets here. I've tried to ring her back, but her phone's turned off.'

'Never mind.' Owen was smiling. 'It's wonderful news!'

'Rather an awkward time to come home!'

'Mmm.' Owen stirred his tea. 'The cottage could be a problem. I'd like to see her clear it out at the moment.' He chuckled.

'Well,' Evie spoke defensively, 'she can't expect us to look after the cottage with so much to do on the farm. After all, it's been nearly a year.'

'She doesn't know about our plans?'

Evie shook her head. 'She's only ever rung from the mobile.' She sighed. 'She was always in a hurry. There never seemed the right opportunity to tell her what was happening here. I thought it better to wait until she came home . . . It'll be a shock to her!'

'Don't worry, dear. We'll sort it out when she arrives.'

He watched his wife thoughtfully. He had done a lot of adjusting lately. He sighed. Not only was his farming life out of control, but his comfortable wife had suddenly undergone an overhaul!

True, she now reminded him of the bright young girl he had met at a Young Farmers' dance all those years ago and he had to admit that, at forty-four, she still had a trim figure. But he wasn't sure about the highlights in her tawny hair, and the last time she'd gone shopping he'd noticed she had worn make-up. It was most disconcerting!

'What's the matter?' Evie shifted uncomfortably under his stare. 'Is my face shiny?'

'Far from it,' Owen replied gruffly. 'You're looking particularly glamorous.'

Evie flushed. 'Well, now things are changing round here I thought it was time I took myself in hand. I don't want to get old before my time.'

'There's no chance of that!'

'Thanks, Owen,' she said gently. 'It's just that I suddenly feel as if we've got in a rut, what with the children and the farm, and it won't hurt us to have a bit of fun occasionally.'

'Are you bored with me?' Owen was worried. Change of any sort bothered him, but this new Evie was alarming.

'Of course I'm not bored! I love you, Owen, and our life together, but a bit of excitement now and then doesn't come amiss.' She smiled at him.

'I think we'll be getting our fair share of that this summer,' Owen muttered and stood up.

'In the meantime,' he planted a kiss on Evie's cheek, 'I must go and see to the cows, they need fresh hay.'

He left the kitchen, leaving Evie

sipping pensively.

Holly Cottage was situated across the lane in a small paddock and had once housed their farm help. Over the years it had been utilised by the children and visiting friends and, for a couple of seasons had been let out as a holiday cottage.

When Kate left school and attended the local Business College she had moved into the cottage to enjoy her independence, as she had called it. Evie smiled wryly as she thought of the piles of washing that had frequently appeared in her kitchen and the meals Kate had continued to demolish but, nevertheless, Evie had been happy with the arrangement.

Then Kate had decided to take time out, had bought a rather dilapidated camper van and disappeared, keeping in touch with infrequent calls.

Now, she expected to return to Holly Cottage! Evie conjured up a picture of the cottage in its present condition and smiled ruefully. Kate was in for a surprise. Quite a lot of changes had taken place this last year.

There had been financial pressures; and Owen had desperately resisted the transition, finally succumbing to the inevitable. Rosa had been a tremendous help, Evie mused. Young she may be, but she had a sensible head on her shoulders and she had been a wonderful ally.

And then, of course there was Ruth Farrell, her friend and neighbour at nearby Hillside Farm. She had been a great source of comfort, if only for lending an ear as Evie poured out her woes.

George, Ruth's husband, had taken a different attitude and a rift had sprung up between Owen and George and that had affected the close friendship between Sam, their son, and her Rosa.

She grimaced and cursed the day that farming became such a worry and that dreaded word 'diversifying' had entered the language. Oh, the problems it caused!

She welcomed the chance to share the burden with Kate and perhaps Kate's business training might now prove useful — if she could be persuaded to stay!

On Hillside Farm, Ruth was tackling George. 'Whether you like it or not, George,' she said determinedly as they sat at the kitchen table having just opened another red bill. 'We're going to have to think of something.'

'Diversifying!' George muttered gloomily. 'I've had Sam on about it all morning.'

'The farm isn't paying,' Ruth continued. 'And now Sam is at home as well, there's just not enough income to keep all three of us.'

George sighed. 'The bull will help.' He was proud of his prize Hereford bull and he hoped it would sire many offspring.

'But not enough' Ruth persisted.

'I suppose you want me to follow Owen's example?' His voice was sarcastic.

'Why not?' Ruth demanded. 'At least

they're facing facts. Evie was saying . . . '

George glared at her. He had noticed a subtle change in her lately. Ever since that darned talk in the village hall on diversifying she had become more dominant. And she had smartened herself up! It was enough to worry a man. They were still young enough to enjoy life, grant you, but he'd always been content with the farm and his family.

Now Ruth had cut her dark hair short and bought some new clothes — and clothes were the last things they could afford. Women! He sighed. If only he could talk to Owen about it . . .

'It's no good you looking like that, George, my lad!' Ruth stood up sharply. 'Evie's my friend and always has been. I'm not shunning her just because you two men are behaving like a pair of squabbling schoolboys. It's about time you patched things up with Owen and apologised.'

'Me, apologise? I think it's Owen

who should apologise.'

'For heaven's sake,' Ruth snapped. 'If you'd come off your high horse, you could learn a thing or two from Owen and his diversifying ideas.'

'Diversifying!' George muttered, picking up the offending bill.

Ruth sighed. Life was so difficult at the moment. She'd done her best to help, taking a part-time job at the bakery; if only Owen wasn't so stubborn . . . She'd have to talk to Sam, perhaps he could make his dad see sense.

The phone rang and Ruth went into the hall. She returned a few minutes later, a worried look on her face.

'That was Doris.'

'Doris?'

'Your sister! She and Jim are thinking of coming over to see us.'

'When?'

'She didn't say. Jim came in, so she said she'd talk to us later.'

Jim and Doris farmed on the coast an hour's drive away and true, they hadn't seen anything of them for quite a while. But what with one thing and another . . .

'I think there's something the matter,' Ruth said.

'Oh?' George sounded alarmed.

'It sounds as if their plans aren't working out.'

'What's happened?'

'I'm not sure.' Ruth stared out of the window. 'Perhaps you'd better ring her back, suggest they come over for a meal tomorrow, it'd be nice to see them.'

George went into the hall, his steps heavy with foreboding. Squaring his shoulders, he picked up the phone.

Back at Stony Ridge Farm, Evie's thoughts were equally glum. What had happened to the simple farming life they had once enjoyed? She had to admit to a certain excitement when she thought about the coming months, but change certainly stirred up emotions and they weren't always good ones.

'Progress!' she muttered. 'Why does it have to be so difficult?'

Heaving herself to her feet and

putting aside her gloomy thoughts, she rinsed the mugs and put away the shopping.

Nothing could be done until she heard from Kate, so there was no point worrying. Young Rosa would be home from school shortly and tonight Evie knew her daughter would be going to the local disco. At sixteen, Rosa was blossoming into an attractive woman and Evie wondered grimly what worries she was going to bring on the family. Even though Owen adored his daughters, Evie couldn't help but feel the responsibility.

George and Ruth were lucky just to have Sam, who was following his father into farming. Evie had discussed the matter with Ruth many times and they always ended up laughing. George and Ruth had been such good friends over the years, until recently.

Her mind shied away from those thoughts and returned to Rosa. She and Sam had been such mates. Now Rosa never mentioned him . . . She would have to speak to Owen again, when the time was right, but the thought of further confrontation made her heart sink.

As the evening approached Kate turned off the motorway and followed familiar signs, singing to herself. She was almost there. Another few miles and she saw the sign to Larchpool.

The village looked the same. Her heart contracted as she drove slowly along the main street. The sound of church bells resonated through the open window and she gave a sigh of pleasure. She had missed her home. The last year had been exciting, tremendous fun, until that last month . . .

Her thoughts drifted back to the romantic days with Danny. She had been so sure he loved her too. It had been an impossibly wonderful winter. She would never forget Christmas. And then . . . Her heart did its usual lurch and she felt the easy tears at the back of her throat.

Determinedly pushing all thoughts of

Daniel to one side, she concentrated on the road. It was over, and now she was nearly home, and that was a blessed relief.

Turning down the lane to Stony Ridge Farm she peered over the hedges. The cattle were grazing peacefully, sheep littered the hills climbing steeply from the backfields and the setting sun mellowed the old stone of the walls.

She would surprise them! She would leave her camper at Holly Cottage and walk across to the farm. She glanced at her watch. They would be eating their evening meal and she would just wander casually in through the door . . . Grinning to herself she turned left into the yard.

The cottage, with its hedges interspersed with variegated holly, looked wonderfully welcoming and she noticed her garden had been tended. Late bulbs bloomed and polyanthus danced gaily in the borders. She was glad to be back. Perhaps now she could get her life in order.

Alighting, she started across the yard. The cottage door opened and a man stepped out. Kate stood still, startled, surveying the stranger. He was tall and rugged, dressed in an open-necked white shirt that fitted snugly into his tight jeans. His dark hair waving untidily over his brow, his blue eyes a startling contrast as they swept coldly over her and beyond to the camper van.

'I'm sorry, we're not open yet.' His rich voice was irritable. 'Come back in May.'

'I beg your pardon?' Kate gasped.

They stared at one another and Kate felt the hackles rise on her neck. He didn't look a lot older than her, but he had an air of confidence and his stance was arrogant. Shivering, she returned his gaze, her own eyes flashing green ice.

This man was dangerous; the thought skimmed the edge of her mind as she took a step forward.

'Who are you?' Her voice was clear in the soft evening air, but inside her

17

stomach churned.

What had happened in her absence? She suddenly regretted turning off her phone and fear made her turn towards Stony Ridge Farm. Had something happened to Mum and Dad?

2

'Who are you?' Kate repeated as she stared at the man in front of her who eyed her warily.

'Grant Drummond.' He took a step forward and held out his hand. 'Miss . . . ?'

Kate ignored the proffered hand and her eyes flicked over him again. 'I'm Kate, Kate Bramwell. My parents own this land.'

'Ah!' His frown cleared and he smiled, relief spreading over his face. 'You're Kate! I see.'

'Well, I'm sure I don't!' Kate retorted. 'Do you mind telling me what's going on?'

'Your parents haven't told you anything?' His gaze was suddenly wary and he narrowed his eyes as he saw her expression. She shook her head.

'They know you're coming home today?'

'Well actually,' she felt colour flame her face, 'they know I'm coming home, but . . .'

'You didn't tell them when,' he finished for her. 'Well, that lets me off the hook anyway,' he added cheerfully and grinned at her. 'Had I known you were arriving I would, of course, have moved out.'

'Oh, would you?' She raised her eyes haughtily. 'You still haven't told me what you're doing here in the first place?'

'I think perhaps your parents ought to explain the situation.' His voice was gentle but his eyes were sparkling with amusement. 'Quite a lot has happened since you took off.'

'So I gather.' Kate spoke defiantly, aware that he had the advantage. 'I didn't expect my cottage to be taken over by a stranger.'

'Your cottage?' he retaliated. 'I wasn't under the impression you owned it?'

Kate glared at him.

'And you expect it to remain empty

for the duration of your travelling?'

Kate flinched at his arrogant tone. 'I thought I might have been consulted,' she snapped.

'Perhaps they couldn't contact you, and long conversations on the mobile are expensive, especially if you're abroad.' His voice was cool and he was looking at her with a certain disdain. Kate felt her anger rising again. The man was insufferable!

'I assure you,' Grant continued. 'I haven't touched your room and its contents. I've merely used the small bedroom for sleeping and the kitchen for meals. Your parents thought it a good idea, as I needed temporary accommodation. I think they thought the cottage would be better maintained if used.'

Kate glowered at him. Everything he said seemed perfectly reasonable, but she was still in shock.

'I'd better go and see Mum and Dad,' she said. 'I take it they are still at the farm?' Her voice was sarcastic but a small tremor of fear touched her skin.

'Of course,' he answered smoothly. 'I think that's an excellent idea. And, should they wish me to vacate the cottage in the morning, tell them I'll be quite happy to make other arrangements.'

He grinned suddenly. 'Of course, if you want to check your belongings,' he waved towards the front door, 'you're welcome to do so now.'

Kate glared at him and, not deigning to reply, stomped back to the camper. Turning sharply on the gravel she shot through the gate and across the lane to Stony Ridge Farm.

Grant stared after her, a thoughtful look on his face and a gleam in his eyes. He could smell trouble! What a shame, he sighed as he re-entered Holly Cottage, everything had been going so smoothly.

In the kitchen at the farm Evie was pouring coffee from a large pot as Rosa carried the plates to the sink. Owen stirred his cup gloomily and Evie sighed.

'Cheer up, Owen.' She forced brightness into her voice. 'Things can only get better.'

Owen grunted sceptically and Rosa grinned. 'Well,' she said, 'I'm looking forward to the summer. I think it will be fun! Larchpool is pretty dead for a village and think of all the tourists milling around. The shops will thrive, the pubs will be bursting at the seams, and it'll be all down to us. We're contributing to the village economy; as well as our own,' she added, laughing.

Owen glared at her. 'All those tourists,' he grumbled. 'That's what I am thinking about.'

'Come on, Dad, lighten up.' Rosa leaned across the table. 'It's only for a few months, and they won't bother you. Mum and I will be doing all the work, and Grant of course. You'll see — it'll be OK.'

Rosa swung her head and her mane of straight dark hair swirled around her shoulders. Brown eyes twinkled as they met the equally dark ones of her father.

She favoured him in looks, whereas Kate resembled her mother.

He was saved from further comment by the sound of a vehicle drawing up in the yard outside.

'Now, who on earth's that?' Evie got to her feet.

'One of those dratted tourists, I expect,' Owen muttered and Evie shot him a quelling glance.

Peering through the window, she let out a cry of delight. 'It's Kate!'

Rosa leapt to her feet and opened the door with a bang. Running across the yard she clasped her sister in a bear-like hug as she stepped down from the camper van.

'Oh, Kate, it's wonderful to see you. I've missed you so much and there's such a lot to tell you!'

'So I gather,' Kate said dryly as she returned the hug. 'Mum!' She kissed her mother.

'It's good to have you home, Kate. Come in, come in. I've just made coffee.'

'Wonderful.' Kate followed her mother in the house, Rosa hanging on to her arm. Her father rose to hug her.

'Welcome home,' he said gruffly and Kate felt her eyes fill with tears.

Greetings over, Kate was tucking into a large slice of her mother's fruit cake. 'Now,' she leaned back and reached for her coffee, 'tell me what's been going on. I went to the cottage and was greeted by a hunk called Grant, who appears to have moved in!' She kept her voice light but Evie saw the anxiety in her daughter's eyes. She cast a beseeching glance at Owen but he refused to look at her and stirred his coffee energetically.

'Well?' Kate looked swiftly from her mother to Rosa. 'Who's going to fill me in then?'

Rosa grinned. 'You're right, he is a hunk!'

'So,' Kate repeated impatiently, 'what's he doing here?'

'It's a long story,' Evie began hesitatingly.

'I'm listening.' Kate relaxed into her chair, watching her mother.

Evie took a deep breath and met her daughter's gaze. 'You know we were suffering because of the foot and mouth epidemic, before you went away,' she said.

'Yes, but I thought you were getting over that. You'd restocked.' Kate's brow furrowed.

'But that cost money,' Evie replied quietly. 'Since the epidemic all we've done is put money into the farm, with very little return. The bottom fell out of the milk market so we decided not to purchase milking cows. The sheep won't come into their own until next year with the lambing and as for the rest, well, we got further and further into debt.'

'But I thought the government were going to help?'

'They were, are, sometime, but all we've done is fill in forms,' Owen interrupted grumpily. 'And still no money.'

26

'Anyway,' Evie continued, 'there was a talk in the village hall, from some minister or other and an agricultural man and Ruth and I went along. They talked a lot of sense about recovery and diversifying.'

Owen snorted.

'It's not a favourite word with Dad.' Rosa grinned.

'To cut a long story short,' Evie said. 'We thought it was a good idea. They sent someone along to assess our assets and they came up with the idea of a campsite.'

'A campsite?' Kate exploded. 'On Stony Ridge?'

'Fun, isn't it?' Rosa giggled.

Owen glared at her.

'They suggested we open up Winterwood Meadow. It's got the woods on either side, the river and, of course, the track runs right down from the main road.'

'Winterwood?' Kate could hardly grasp the implications. Winterwood Meadow, situated as it was amongst the firs and great oaks with the Larch river cascading over the boulders, was her haven. A dell of peace, with wild flowers and birdsong . . . Winterwood — a campsite? She looked at her mother in horror.

Evie sighed at her daughter's reaction; she could have anticipated it, Kate was so much like her father in temperament.

'So,' she continued brightly, 'that's what we're doing. Opening a campsite, on the first of May. The toilet block is complete and there's a small shop. I shall run that and Rosa will help in the holidays.'

Kate collected her chaotic thoughts. 'So where does Grant fit into all this?'

'Ah, Grant.' Evie smiled. 'He's been absolutely wonderful. He's employed by the Small Business Initiative who helped us plan and set this up. Grant obtained all the permissions and did the necessary paperwork. He's also organised the entire building work and site layout. We couldn't have done it without him.'

'And my cottage?'

'Well, he's supervising several schemes around here and he needed temporary accommodation. As the cottage was empty, it seemed an ideal way to keep it aired.'

'I see.' Kate looked woebegone. 'I do think you might have told me!'

'How could we?' Evie shrugged. 'You didn't contact us very often, and then you used your mobile. The signal was often poor and you seemed to be enjoying yourself, so there was no point in worrying you.'

Kate looked uncomfortable. 'If I'd known I could have come home sooner.'

'What for? There was nothing you could have done, we'd have had to pay Grant then, whereas . . . '

'You don't pay Grant?' Kate asked suspiciously.

'He comes as part of the grant we get for diversifying,' Evie explained. 'We should have paid him a small wage, but he insisted that free accommodation would be equal to that.'

'So, what does Grant get out of it?'

'It's his job,' her mother replied.

'I take it you've checked all this out?' Kate turned to her father, who merely shrugged. 'It sounds very dodgy to me.'

'Kate,' Evie said firmly. 'You've been away for nearly a year, doing what you wanted. In that time, we've had to cope with a financial crisis. We have and so far, we're still able to keep the farm. It's lovely to have you home, but please take time to assess the situation before you criticise. Now,' her voice softened, 'have some more coffee and tell us all about your travels.'

Kate passed her cup, her thoughts in turmoil.

'We'll discuss it again tomorrow,' Evie said. 'Your bed's made up in your old room, so you can sleep here tonight. Tomorrow we'll talk about the future and what you intend to do.'

Kate had to be content with that and, for the next hour, she regaled them with tales of her travels. She didn't mention Danny and, as she tossed and turned in the familiar bed, her thoughts were far from relaxed.

Dozing fitfully, Kate woke as the grey dawn filtered through the curtains. She lay for a moment assembling her thoughts and then dressed quickly. Creeping downstairs she could hear her mother in the kitchen. Her father would be out seeing to the stock before breakfast. Quietly she let herself out of the side door and set off down the lane.

The birds were calling in the trees and the young shoots in the hedgerows sparkled with dew. She felt her heart lift. Finally she stood at the gate to Winterwood Meadow. It was a new gate of gleaming wood, freshly varnished, and it swung open easily to her touch. The meadow spread before her, the wind soughing in the fir trees and the river sloshing as it cascaded over the rocky bed.

She gazed around. To the right there was a small wooden building, the new shop she guessed, and farther down the hedge lattice fencing hid another building. Neither was intrusive to the peace. She wandered farther into the field. The grass was short at this time of year although it now looked smoothly mown and she noted numbers nailed to wooden posts at regular intervals around the perimeter.

Thoughtfully she retraced her steps and entered the kitchen to the welcome smell of frying bacon.

'Kate, you're up early.' Evie was busy over the Aga. 'I thought you'd be tired after all your travelling.'

'I couldn't sleep,' Kate admitted and Evie glanced at her shrewdly.

'It won't do any harm to try this venture, you know,' she said as she split eggshells. 'We can always revert if it doesn't work out.'

Kate smiled and poured herself a mug of tea.

'I know, Mum,' she said. 'it was just such a shock to come home to such a transition. I'd thought . . . '

'That we'd all be sitting here where you left us!' Evie finished for her.

'Times change, Kate. And we had to think of something to save the farm. Think how you'd have felt if you'd come back to a 'For Sale' sign!'

Kate grinned. 'OK. I give in.'

'Besides,' Evie glanced at her with a wry smile, 'despite what your father feels, I'm enjoying the situation.'

'You are?' Kate stared at her mother.

'I am!' Evie grinned. 'It's all rather exciting. I'm looking forward to running the shop and meeting all these new people. Just think, holiday-makers from all over the country, even abroad! It'll make life in Larchpool more fun, don't you think?'

Kate mulled over her mother's words. She hadn't really thought about her mum's life on the farm. She was quite isolated, with only the locals for company.

She studied her mother. She did look different. It was probably the hairdo but, somehow, she looked younger. And she was attractive, Kate acknowledged. She had never thought of her mother in this light and it made her slightly uncomfortable. Mum was Mum, after all, but she was still entitled to a life of her own.

'Let's talk about you, Kate, have you any idea what you want to do now you're home?'

Kate shook her head. 'I imagine you'll need some help here?'

'We can't pay you.'

Kate shrugged. 'I managed to save some of my earnings while I was abroad. If I get something part-time, I'll be able to help out as well.'

'We'll see.' Evie was non-committal.

'About Holly Cottage,' Kate hesitated and her mother glanced at her, 'I don't mind staying here for a while, and I've got the camper. If I can fetch some of my clothes . . . '

'It would help,' Evie answered gratefully. 'Grant won't be here much longer and it would save any delay to the scheme if he had to move.'

'Then that's what I'll do,' Kate said. 'I'll go and see Grant after breakfast.'

Kate approached the cottage with trepidation. For some reason she felt nervous. Bracing herself, she opened the gate and then stopped short in surprise. A gleaming back Mercedes was parked outside the back door. Surely that wasn't Grant's? She searched her memory and she was sure it hadn't been in the yard the previous night when she arrived. Reaching the door, she knocked loudly and turned to stare again at the luxurious vehicle.

The door opened sharply. 'Oh, Kate!' There was no welcome in Grant's eyes; indeed he looked positively uncomfortable.

'I need to talk to you, Grant.' Kate peered past him into the kitchen. She could see several men seated around the table, staring in her direction.

'I'm in a business meeting.' His voice was cold. 'It's rather inconvenient. Could you come back later?'

Without waiting for an answer he shut the door and Kate stared at the blank wood, her mouth open.

'How very rude!' she muttered and, turning on her heel, marched out of the yard. Well, she would think again about giving up her cottage.

'That was unfortunate,' the older man at the table drawled. 'Shall we get back to business?'

Grant grimaced and glanced through the window at Kate's retreating back. Unfortunate indeed! Inside he cursed, but when he turned back to the table there was a smile on his face, a smile that didn't reach his eyes.

'Shall we continue, Gentlemen?'

3

Kate marched into the kitchen and reached for the kettle. Her mother looked at her stormy expression in surprise.

'What's the matter with you?'

'Grant's visitors,' Kate muttered and spooned coffee into a mug. 'I'll have to go back later.'

'Oh,' Evie carried on peeling potatoes, 'He often has business meetings.'

'What do you really know about him, Mum?'

Her mother frowned. 'Not a lot, I suppose,' she said thoughtfully. 'The Small Business Initiative sent him along. He's been a tremendous help.' She glanced at her daughter. 'We couldn't have done anything without him.'

'But do you trust him?'

'Of course! He's discussed every

move with your father, so we know exactly what's going on. Even the contract didn't seem quite so alarming when he explained it.'

'The contract? You've signed a contract?'

Her mother sighed and turned round. 'Look, Kate, I appreciate your concern, but this has been going on for months. We're aware of all the pitfalls and we know what we're doing.'

'I hope so,' Kate murmured. 'You've got a solicitor?'

'Not at the moment. We've no need for one,' Evie said. 'Solicitors are expensive and we've tried to be as economical as we can. Now,' she banged the saucepan lid, 'stop worrying. I'm sure your father will go through all the paperwork with you if you like, to put your mind at rest.'

Kate stirred her coffee and stared into the swirling liquid. Try as she might, she couldn't help the unease that clouded her mind. She didn't want to upset her parents but she was going to find out more about Grant, by whatever means it took!

At that moment the image of her thoughts rapped the door. Kate met his smile with a frown.

'Kate,' his voice was warm, 'I'm sorry about earlier. We had a business meeting. You want to talk to me?'

'Come in, Grant,' Evie called. 'Coffee?'

'I'd love one.' Grant stared pointedly at Kate and reluctantly she opened the door for him to pass. Seated at the table he leaned back, his eyes twinkling.

'You want to move back into the cottage?' he guessed.

Kate frowned again. He really was an attractive man, and immaculate again in a sparkling white shirt that clung to his tight-fitting jeans. She felt her defences rise. He was too attractive by half and the charm he was portraying was obviously a useful tool. But she was not going to be taken in. After Daniel, she didn't trust any man!

'Actually, no,' she said coolly. 'I've discussed it with Mum and she seems to think you'll be moving out shortly anyway.'

Grant raised his eyebrows and glanced at Evie.

'So, for convenience sake, and to expedite your departure, I've agreed to stay here for now. I would appreciate it if I could collect some of my things from my room; otherwise, the cottage is all yours.'

Kate was aware that her speech sounded stilted and unfriendly and she coloured at the amusement that sparkled from his blue eyes.

'Of course,' he replied smoothly. 'Would now be a suitable time?'

'Thank you.' Kate downed her. coffee. 'I'll just get a bag.'

She disappeared from the kitchen and Evie gave Grant a rueful smile.

'You must excuse my daughter, Grant. The changes have come as a shock to her and she feels guilty that she hasn't been here to help.'

'Of course.' Grant flashed his disarming smile. 'It's perfectly natural. She probably thinks I'm taking over the farm and going to throw you out into the street!'

Kate returned to the sound of their laughter and gazed at them suspiciously.

'Shall we go?' Grant unwound his tall frame from the chair and held open the door.

Disgruntled, Kate stepped out into the yard. She knew it was her own fault that she hadn't been included in the new plans, but she hated the feeling of exclusion. Anyone would think she'd been away for years!

She glowered at Grant and followed him to Holly Cottage. He opened the front door with a flourish and his eyes were amused as she headed for the stairs.

'Take your time,' he called after her. 'I'll put the kettle on.'

Kate gazed around her old room. True to his word, Grant had disturbed nothing. Sorting her clothes quickly, she packed her bag and took a last look.

The remainder could stay until she returned. Hopefully that wouldn't be too long. Carting her bag downstairs she found Grant in the kitchen. He handed her a steaming mug.

'All in order?' He perched on a stool and his gaze swept disconcertingly over her face.

'All fine,' she said stiffly. 'I've got all I need for now.'

'Good.' He stared at her for a moment. 'Kate, do you think we could drop the antagonism? If you're going to help out and take over the running of the business side we shall need to work together.'

'Take over the business?' Kate was startled.

'Ah, your father hasn't spoken to you yet?'

Kate shook her head and stared at him.

'Well, I gather you went to business college before you set off touring?'

She nodded.

'It would seem logical that you would

be able to do the paperwork, book-keeping, records and so on.' He gestured across the room and Kate saw a computer set up near the window. 'Everything's computerised of course and, unless you want to employ someone, we thought you would be ideal to take over when I leave.'

'Which will be when?'

Grant shrugged. 'It's difficult to tell. The site opens in May so, hopefully, soon after.'

'I see.' Kate thought for a moment.

'I'll go through everything with you,' Grant's voice was smooth, 'and you'll pay yourself a salary . . . ' He held up his hand as she started to protest. 'It will be put against tax and therefore will help. Besides,' he grinned suddenly and she felt her heart somersault as his twinkling eyes held hers, 'unless you made a fortune on your travels, you'll need an income.'

She felt the heat rise in her cheeks and stared at the computer. 'I'll need to think about this,' she muttered.

'Of course!' His voice was cool again as he rose. 'Discuss it with your father. There's no hurry.'

'Except that you want to leave.'

He shrugged. 'I can't do that yet,' he said. 'I've other projects in the area that haven't got off the ground yet.'

'Such as?' She couldn't help being curious.

'Similar diversifying, some bed and breakfast, a nursery with organic vegetables; for Stony Ridge a campsite seemed the better option.'

Kate had to agree there. She could just imagine if her mother had decided to do bed and breakfast — strangers in the bathroom? She grinned involuntarily and Grant raised an eyebrow.

'Sorry. I was just imagining Dad with lodgers!'

'Ah, yes,' he smiled, 'not quite his thing.'

He picked up her bag. 'Can you manage this or shall I carry it back to the farm?'

'I can manage, thank you,' she replied firmly.

For a moment their fingers touched and she felt a tingle through her hand. This was ridiculous! She couldn't be attracted to this man. For a start, she didn't trust him and for another thing, he couldn't wait to leave! One heartache was enough.

In the doorway of Holly Cottage Grant watched her, a pensive look in his eyes. He found her attractive and he couldn't help but admire the way she was suspicious for her family. Owen was gullible and Evie, delightful though she was, was very naïve when it came to business. He sighed. Neither of them had questioned his trustworthiness and he felt the familiar unease creep into his mind.

If Kate started probing . . . Shaking his head he went back to the computer and stared moodily at the screen. The sooner Winterwood Site was up and running the better. It was inconceivable that he should become emotionally involved with the family, and as for Kate . . . He smiled wryly, his heart softening.

Kate unpacked slowly, her thoughts troubled. Getting used to the innovations would be no problem. Now her mother had explained the circumstances and she had inspected Winterwood, she was quite happy with the idea. In fact, like Evie, she could see that running the business would be fun. She was quite prepared to give it a go, once Grant had instructed her. But there was the problem — Grant.

Well, there was only one way to find out if she had any cause to be concerned. She would speak to her father, offer to take over the running of the site and take a look at the administration herself. Anything untoward would soon be apparent. Satisfied that action was the best plan she ran downstairs to the kitchen. Her mother was mixing a cake.

'Where's Dad?'

'Gone into Larchpool. It's market day.'

'Of course!' Kate was disappointed.

'Why, dear, is there something the matter?'

'No, nothing the matter,' Kate replied. 'I've just been talking to Grant. He seems to think it would be a good idea if I took over the administration of the business.'

'I think that's a marvellous idea.' Evie smiled approvingly. 'It would be wonderful, working together as a family. And it would save having to employ someone.'

'Technically, I shall be employed,' Kate said. 'I'll draw a small salary, as will you, Mum, if you run the shop.'

'That'll be nice!' Evie grinned. 'What about your father? Can he be paid too?'

'I imagine he'll be a director.' Kate frowned. 'Anyway, I need to have a word with Dad, get his go-ahead, and then I'll sort everything out with Grant.'

'What will you sort out with Grant?' Rosa wandered into the kitchen in her dressing-gown. Saturday was her 'flake-out' day, as she called it. She reached for the coffee pot.

'Running Winterwood Site,' Kate

47

said. 'You've no objection?'

'Fantastic!' Rosa beamed. 'Oh, it's all going to be really cool!'

'And hard work,' Kate warned.

Kate watched her younger sister fondly. 'And what about you, Rosa? What's been happening in your life while I've been away?'

'Not a lot!' Rosa grimaced. 'School, tests, all the usual stuff. At least I shall pack up early this year, as it's my last.'

'You 'pack up early' as you put it, to revise for your exams in June,' her mother said sternly. 'And tourists or not, you'll be doing your revision.'

'Yes, Mum,' Rosa sighed. 'But I'll be able to help out some of the time. All work and no play . . .

'And who's the latest heartthrob?' Kate teased. 'Is Sam still top of your dating list?'

Rosa frowned at Kate and glanced at her mother. Evie was concentrating on spooning her cake mix into baking tins.

'Well?' Kate persisted.

'Of course I still like Sam.' Rosa

drummed her fingers on the table. 'It's Dad. Since he and George fell out, it's been . . . difficult.'

'Ruth is still my best friend,' said Evie firmly. 'I haven't stopped seeing her just because the two men are behaving like spoilt children.'

'But Sam's not welcome here any more,' Rosa said quietly. 'You know that yourself, Mum, and somehow Dad makes me feel disloyal every time I mention him!'

'You shouldn't allow their squabble to spoil your friendship with Sam,' Evie said, banging the oven door shut.

'What on earth have they fallen out over?' Kate had been listening to the conversation in amazement. 'They've been friends all their lives, grown up together, farmed together; how can they possibly have fallen out?'

'It's all to do with this diversifying.' Evie sighed. 'I wasn't there at the time, neither was Ruth, so we don't know exactly what happened. All we know is that, suddenly, we had two very angry men who totally disrupted a lifetime of friendship, and neither will explain or apologise.'

'Isn't there anything we can do?' Kate was aghast.

'Until we know precisely what the row was about, there's not a lot anyone can do!'

'We've all tried talking, even being angry,' Rosa said. 'But neither of the silly blighters will budge. So we've learned to live with it.'

'Ridiculous!' Kate snorted.

She was getting more and more disconcerted at what had happened while she had been away. Thank goodness her plans with Daniel had gone awry, otherwise she wouldn't have been at home right now and heaven only knew what else she would discover in the next few days!

It was evening before Kate had a chance to speak to her father. Evie and Rosa had gone into the sitting-room to watch a television programme and Owen settled himself by the Aga in the kitchen with a mug of cocoa.

'Dad, I need to talk to you.'

Her father surveyed her thoughtfully. 'Aye, I thought you might,' he said resignedly. 'Fire away.'

Kate suppressed a smile. 'Right, I spoke to Grant this morning.' Owen gazed into the fire watching the sparks from the logs spatter against the glass. When the silence lengthened he turned to his daughter.

'And?' he prompted.

'Well, Grant suggested I take over the administration and accounts of the project.'

'That sounds like a perfectly sensible idea.' Owen's voice was bland.

'You've no objection?'

'Someone's got to do it and I don't fancy some stranger nosing around in my affairs.'

'So I can get Grant to show me the ropes.'

'Feel free!' Owen's voice was suddenly bitter.

'Dad, you know it's for the best.'

Kate's voice was gentle as she leaned towards him. 'You'd hate to have to sell the farm and it's a better idea than bed and breakfast, for instance.'

Owen glared at her. 'You don't have to convince me, lass, they've all been at the sweet talk for months.' He sighed. 'I've agreed to the site because I know it's the only way out,' he took a sip of his cocoa, 'that doesn't mean I've got to like it.' He sounded grumpy.

'It will make it a lot easier if you could at least be pleasant about it,' Kate said. 'It's going to be hard work for us all, especially Mum, and she'd be so much happier if you wouldn't be such a grouch!'

'I do try, lass, but 'tis awfully wearing.'

'It's even more wearing for Mum,' Kate replied quickly. 'Let's all try and work together, eh, Dad? Just for the summer, and then we can assess the situation in the autumn and decide where to go next.'

'All right.' Owen reached forward

and patted her knee. 'I'll try, lass, I really will. It's been such a difficult time.' He stared sadly into the flames. 'I guess I've been a bit selfish,' Kate raised her eyebrows, 'all right, more than a bit.' He grinned ruefully. 'I'll do my best to help out too.'

'That's all I'm asking, Dad,' Kate said, relieved. 'That's all I'm asking. That you work with us, not against.'

Father and daughter sat quietly for a few minutes each lost in thought.

'Dad,' Kate hesitated as her father looked up. 'About you and George . . . '

Owen's face darkened. 'I'll not be talking about that man!' he said abruptly and glared warningly at Kate.

'OK, Dad.' Kate's heart sank. One hurdle at a time, she told herself.

'It's nought to do with anyone else,' her father went on in a softer tone. 'It's between me and George, and it's not easy to forgive.'

'Forgive what?'

'Tis no good raking it all up again,' Owen said. 'Until he comes and says he's sorry, I don't even want to think about the man.'

'I'm away to bed.' Kate kissed her father's forehead and left the kitchen.

'Men,' she muttered to herself. Would she ever understand them?

At that moment Rosa was asking herself the same question as she slipped out of the back door and headed for the barn. This furtive creeping about was against her nature and she was angry with the men who made it a necessity.

The door creaked open again and a figure was silhouetted against the moonlight.

'Sam, is that you?' she whispered, a shiver touching the hairs on the back of her neck.

4

'Sam, is that you?' Rosa repeated, her heart hammering. She was nervous enough about the forbidden meeting.

'Of course it's me, silly.' Sam strode across the hay-strewn floor, his fair hair unruly from the night wind. He pulled her to him. Muffled against his shoulder she let out a sigh.

'This can't go on, Sam. I hate this creeping about at night.'

'So, what do you want to do?'

They sat together on a hay bale, their arms entwined and Sam stroked her cheek.

'I'll do whatever you want, you know that,' he said gently. 'I'm not keen on this subterfuge either. Mum knows we meet, but Dad would have a fit at the moment and I don't think I can bear the thought of not seeing you.'

'I know. But I think it's time we took

a stand. I thought this silly row would blow over, but there's no sign of that. I don't suppose your dad has said anything?' Her voice was hopeful but she felt Sam shake his head in the darkness.

'Nothing,' he replied sadly. 'Every time I mention Stony Ridge he goes all grumpy and walks out!'

'Dad's the same. Whatever was it all about?'

'Heaven only knows! Something to do with your campsite, I think.'

'Anyway, whatever the cause, it's about time things were sorted out. I know it's worrying Mum. She's still friends with your mum of course, they meet in town, but the atmosphere is terrible at home and what with the new site and Dad all grumpy . . . By the way, Kate's home.'

'Is she? Oh, that's great. Perhaps she'll make them see sense.'

'Umm.' Rosa sounded doubtful. 'She and Dad are very close and she's going to work at home for a while . . . In the meantime,' her voice became determined, 'I'm not going to hide our meetings any more.'

'Oh.' Sam's heart sank. Much as he cared for Rosa he hated confrontation and he was quite prepared to sit things out until their respective fathers saw sense, but Rosa was a very determined lady!

'I'm not creeping out at nights any more,' Rosa said. 'From now on we meet in Larchpool and if Dad's angry then that's his problem.'

She thought for a moment. Her father seemed permanently angry at the moment, so her meeting Sam shouldn't make that much difference. She was sure her mother would back her stance; Evie certainly hadn't tried to hide the fact that she still met Ruth, and this clandestine behaviour was extremely uncomfortable.

'Right.' Sam tried to match her enthusiasm. 'I'm game if you are. So, where do we go from here?'

'There's a good film showing at the

cinema,' Rosa replied. 'Tomorrow night I'll meet you outside at half-past five. That'll give us time to see the film, go for a coffee and then we can catch the last bus home. Deal?'

'Deal,' he agreed.

Rosa heard the doubt in his voice.

'You will be there?' she asked anxiously. She realised she was testing his commitment to her and her heart gave a flutter.

'Of course, I'll be there,' he said gruffly. 'Outside the cinema at five-thirty. I promise.'

He gave her a long lingering kiss and she slipped quietly back into the farmyard. Sam began the trek across the field to Hillside, relief that he wouldn't have to make the dark journey again tempered with misgivings as he thought of his father's reaction to his plans.

The next morning dawned clear and bright. 'Only two weeks to go,' Evie said at breakfast. 'And then the invasion starts!'

Owen grunted and spooned marmalade on to his toast.

Kate smiled. 'I thought I'd go and have a word with Grant,' she said. 'The sooner I get started on the admin, the better. That is, if he doesn't mind working on a Sunday?'

'He seems to work every day,' her mother replied. 'I shouldn't think he'd mind at all.'

'Is everything ready?' Kate asked.

'As far as I know,' Evie replied. 'The basic goods for the shop are arriving some time this week. Fresh produce is organised and the bakery and milkman will deliver daily.'

'And reception, where will the tourists book in?'

'I'm putting the desk in the corner of the kitchen,' Evie replied. 'It's big enough and the campers have to come through the yard. There'll be a large sign telling them to call at the house on their way to the site and I've got a field map that will show where everyone is sited.'

'Very professional!' Kate smiled approvingly.

'There'll also be local information and leaflets, and we'll take it from there. The first summer is going to be a bit trial and error but, by the end of the season, we should be well organised for the future.'

'If there are more seasons!' Owen muttered crossly.

'Dad!' Kate said warningly. 'Remember your promise.'

Her mother raised an eyebrow. 'Promise?'

Kate grinned. 'Dad has promised to be more positive,' she said. 'Haven't you, Dad?'

Owen grunted and cast a baleful glance at his family. 'I suppose so,' he agreed as they all stared at him. 'I'll try.'

'Good,' said Evie briskly as she started to clear the table. 'That's all we ask.'

She turned to her younger daughter. 'You're quiet this morning, Rosa. Are you all right?'

Rosa mumbled something and stood up. 'I'll help you wash up, Mum.'

'You will?' said Evie in surprise and then met her daughter's gaze. 'Oh, fine, yes thank you, that will be a help.'

Owen excused himself and, putting on his boots, disappeared through the back door.

'Well, Rosa?'

Rosa swirled the water for a moment and then took a deep breath. 'It's Sam, Mum. I'm meeting him tonight.'

'Oh, I see.' Evie looked thoughtful. 'And when was this arranged?'

'Last night,' Rosa whispered. 'I'm sorry, Mum. I've been seeing Sam secretly. You know what Dad's like at the moment. Only . . . ' She glanced at her mother's face. 'Only I don't like being underhand and we've decided to come out in the open. We're going to the cinema and then I'll catch the last bus home.'

'Well, I'm glad you've decided to be honest at last.'

'You knew?'

'I guessed,' Evie said gently. 'You were both too close to suddenly stop being friends. You could have told me, you know.'

'I know, Mum. But there was so much going on and you've had enough to worry about. I thought it would be easier . . . '

'Anyway,' Evie planted a kiss on her daughter's dark head, 'I'm glad you've told me now. And you know you have my support. I won't let your father's silly quarrel spoil my friendship with Ruth so why should it affect you and Sam?'

'Thanks, Mum.'

'Your father will come round eventually. He'll have to,' said Evie. 'In the meantime, I shall be a lot happier knowing where you are and that you're with Sam. So, you go off and enjoy yourselves. I'll deal with your father.'

'Thanks, Mum, I knew I could count on you.' Giving her mother a big hug Rosa ran from the kitchen and Evie heard her pounding up the stairs.

'Hey,' Evie called. 'What about the washing up?'

But she was smiling as she plunged her hands into the soapy water. Finishing the clearing up she picked up the phone.

'Ruth? It's Evie. Are you on your own?'

She heard Ruth chuckle as she replied in the affirmative. 'This takes me back to my youth!' Ruth laughed. 'Trying to talk to boyfriends while the parents were out of the way.'

'I know! No such thing as mobiles then. Are you still on for tomorrow?'

'Of course,' Ruth replied. 'I'm looking forward to it. We'll go shopping and then lunch. Agreed?'

'Rather! I'm looking for some new shoes. Now the dances have started up in the village hall I'm hoping to persuade Owen to go occasionally. He always used to enjoy dancing.'

'We all did,' Ruth agreed. 'And it's time we started having a bit of a social life. If we can't cajole the men into going, we'll go by ourselves.'

Evie giggled. 'That would give the gossips something to talk about. By the way, I've had a chat to Rosa this morning.'

'She told you about her and Sam?' Ruth sounded relieved.

'You knew?'

'I tackled him last night. I heard him sneaking out and was worried. I told him it's not an acceptable way to behave, so I'm glad they've come out into the open. Owen and George will just have to get used to the idea. Why should their petty squabbles affect the youngsters?'

'I agree with you entirely. They didn't object to their friendship before, and I won't have their stubbornness driving them to secret meetings. It's very worrying.'

'Never mind, we'll cheer ourselves up tomorrow. Not that I've got much money to spend, but I can always dream!' Ruth sighed as she replaced the receiver. Without Evie's cheerful friendship she wasn't sure how she would have survived the last few weeks. As it was . . .

Determinedly she pushed her gloomy thoughts aside and started on the lunch.

Back at Stony Ridge Kate approached Holly Cottage with trepidation. She didn't feel in the mood for dealing with Grant yet, but the sooner she got started the better. Knocking on the door, which was ajar, she waited. There was no sound.

'Grant?' she called but there was still no response. Pushing the door slowly open and calling his name again she entered the kitchen. The room was warm and there was a mug of coffee on the table. Grant was obviously about. Making her way across the room to the computer she noticed a large yellow folder on the table.

Leaning over she read the label. GDP Ltd glared at her in large black letters. She was about to open the folder when she heard a noise and looked up. Grant was standing in the doorway, his expression harsh. His eyes flew from her face to the folder and she saw his jaw tighten.

'Did you want something?' His voice was angry and his blue eyes sparked ice.

'Sorry.' Kate felt distinctly uncomfortable. 'I did knock and call and the door was open.'

'Did you want something?' he repeated, his voice softer but his eyes were wary.

'I thought that, if you didn't mind, we could make a start on the admin,' Kate said, angry at her disadvantage. 'Dad seems to think it's a good idea and, as we're opening in a couple of weeks, I thought the sooner the better.'

He moved into the room and picked up the folder. For a moment he studied it as if trying to gauge whether it had been opened and then, apparently satisfied, he placed it in a drawer, which he closed and locked. Only then did he turn and look at Kate.

'Of course,' he said smoothly, the anger erased from his expression. 'That's an excellent idea. Would you like a coffee?'

He turned to the kettle as she nodded and let out a sigh of relief. Somehow she had felt herself in a very dangerous position, but whatever the situation had been it had passed and she was left feeling distinctly uneasy.

However the morning passed pleasantly and Kate was agreeably surprised by the set-up, spreadsheets ready to be completed, a straightforward accounts package that had been tailored to their business. After two hours she leaned back in her chair and stretched her arms.

'This all looks great,' she said.

'Good, I'm glad you approve.' She looked at him quickly but there was a bland smile on his face. 'I suggest you come in each morning and familiarise yourself with the details. Stock for the shop will be arriving shortly, so if you start on that immediately, there'll be no backlog and everything can be accounted for.'

Kate nodded her head in agreement. 'Sounds good,' she said. 'Shall we say nine each morning? Then you can make arrangements to let me in.'

'I'll show you where I keep the key' Grant said.

'As long as you trust me?' Kate said lightly.

'Is there any reason why I shouldn't?' He studied her intently.

'No, of course not!' Uncomfortable under his gaze she got to her feet. 'Do you have the paperwork, contracts and so on?'

'In that cupboard there.' He indicated a small filing cabinet. 'I'll leave the key on the desk and you can go through it all tomorrow.'

Leaving the cottage, she wandered slowly back to the farm. It seemed obvious to her that Grant was hiding something, but without any proof, it was impossible to say anything.

For some reason her doubts left her feeling extremely miserable. She had enjoyed working alongside him and, when the tension between them disappeared, they seemed in rather sweet harmony.

In Holly Cottage, Grant opened the filing cabinet and took out the pile of papers. Grimly he started to sort through them, selecting several and packaging them separately. As he worked, Kate's face appeared in his mind and he sighed.

'Women,' he muttered. They were a pain. The sooner he moved on again the better. He had no intention of ever getting involved in a serious relationship. He had seen what marriage had done to his father . . .

The following morning Kate arrived punctually at Holly Cottage. There was no sign of Grant. Relieved, she found the key and let herself in. Settling at the computer she switched it on and browsed through the accounts. There were very few entries and all appeared banal.

Listening for a few minutes and convinced of her solitude, she logged on to the Internet and put out a search for GDP Ltd. The motor ticked and then a website appeared. Clicking the mouse again she entered and there unfolded details of the company she had been searching for. Gooding Development Projects Ltd — a company who portrayed itself as a philanthropic firm, reclaiming waste ground and putting it to community use.

They also owned a string of commercial camping and caravanning sites. There was a picture of the director, Harry Gooding, and Kate stared long and hard at the smiling face. Hearing a sound outside she quickly printed out the information — there was very little, one page covering the brief details — and stuffed it into her handbag.

As she closed the Internet and reverted to the accounts she heard the door open. She felt the colour rise in her cheeks as she turned to greet Grant.

'Hi,' she said brightly, aware of his intent gaze.

He stared first at Kate and then at the computer. A gleam of speculation lit his eyes.

'Everything all right?' he asked quietly.

'Everything's fine,' she answered

quickly and closed down the computer. 'I was just finishing actually.'

He didn't detain her as she picked up her bag and headed through the door but, as he watched her cross the yard, his expression was thoughtful and he turned back and switched the computer on again.

Annoyed with herself, Kate ran straight to her room. Talk about giving the game away! Her intention had been to study the paper documents the first time she had been alone, and she had blown that opportunity!

She really must try and be more controlled. She had nothing to be embarrassed about and it was her job to sort the admin and understand it all. Tomorrow she would be more confident.

Straightening her shoulders she took the papers from her handbag and studied the details she had acquired about GDP. Why should Grant be interested in this company?

Harry Gooding grinned complacently at her and she studied it for some

71

time before shrugging and slipping it into a drawer. The man looked pleasant enough, but there was unease on the edge of her mind that she couldn't explain.

5

Evie and Ruth were enjoying cheese-cake after spending the morning browsing round the shops.

'I think it's about time we started having a social life again,' Ruth said thoughtfully. 'We haven't been out for ages and now they're starting monthly dances in the village, I think we should go.' Her voice was wistful.

'Then let's,' Evie replied. 'The first one is on the Saturday after we open the site so how about it?'

'Will you have the time?'

'I'll make time! We've only three bookings so far. We shan't get really busy until the schools' half-term. I'm sure none of our campers will expect us to be available twenty-four hours a day. Perhaps they'll come to the dance as well!'

'Fantastic, it's a date. But what about the men?' Ruth grimaced.

'What about them? We'll tell them we're going. It's up to them whether they come or not. Someone's got to make a stand in this stupid situation and I don't intend to let their silly rift spoil the rest of my life!'

'I agree,' Ruth said. 'If they won't come, we'll go by ourselves, that'll shock them!'

Laughing, they paid the bill and headed for home. At that moment confrontation seemed like a good idea but, as Evie opened the farmhouse door, she felt her heart sink as she heard Owen in the kitchen.

'Good day out?' he asked cheerfully, pouring boiling water into the teapot.

'Very.' Evie smiled and kissed him on the cheek. 'We put the world to rights,' she added lightly.

'No shopping?' Owen looked surprised and Evie shook her head.

'I didn't see anything I liked,' she replied. 'Besides I haven't much spare cash at the moment. Perhaps when the site opens . . . '

Owen didn't respond, as he put two mugs on the table.

'Did you know they're starting dances at Larchpool Hall again?' Evie watched Owen's reaction as she sipped her tea.

'Really?'

'Ruth and I thought it would be nice to go. It's ages since we went out and enjoyed ourselves. It would be such fun,' she added as Owen frowned into his drink. 'Can we go?'

'Will George be going?'

'Of course,' Evie said smoothly. 'It's time you two buried the hatchet. Surely you can socialise for one night?'

'We're not going if George is,' Owen said forcefully and glared at Evie.

'Well,' Evie stood up, 'you might not go, but I certainly am!' And, with that, she stalked out of the kitchen, leaving Owen staring at the slammed door in amazement.

Finally opening day dawned. Evie breathed a sigh of relief as she peered out of the window. A watery sun was

75

piercing the clouds and a slight breeze lifted the young shoots on the trees. It seemed important for the first day to be perfect!

Choosing her clothes with care, she surveyed herself in the mirror — tailored jeans, and a light jumper of lemon yellow, which accentuated the highlights in her tawny hair and showed off her still-youthful figure to advantage.

'Not bad!' she muttered to herself. Smiling, she went downstairs and poured herself coffee. Owen had been about for over an hour and she saw the debris of his breakfast littering the table. Clearing up quickly she crossed to the desk and checked everything was ready. Satisfied, she opened the back door. Now all she needed was a tourist!

She consulted her diary — one booking for today, a Mr Millington. Well, no doubt he would arrive in his own time. Sighing, she returned to the kitchen as Kate made an appearance.

'Well, Mum,' she said, grinning. 'This is it!'

At mid-morning Owen appeared for a coffee.

'No tourists yet?' he asked, reaching for a mug.

Before Evie could reply, she heard the sound of an engine in the yard. Trying not to appear too eager, she waited for the doorbell to chime. Opening it with a smile of welcome she prepared to greet her first guest.

'You must be Mr Millington?'

The tall man smiled at her and she had an immediate impression of a likeable face with twinkling brown eyes. Dark hair, slightly greying at the temples was swept back neatly and his handshake was firm.

'Come in, Mr Millington.' Evie held open the door and he followed her.

'Jack, please.' He flashed her a wide smile.

'What a charming house,' he exclaimed, looking around. 'I'm sure I'm going to enjoy my stay here. And such a delightful welcome!' He bowed slightly before he sat and Evie felt the colour flood her face. Behind her, she heard a muttered oath as Owen banged his mug on the table.

'Thank you,' Evie said hurriedly. 'If I could just have a few details?'

Jack Millington put her at her ease within moments. He was travelling alone, would be staying for two weeks and would park his camper van wherever she suggested.

'The choice is yours,' Evie said, smiling. 'You're our first guest so you can park under the trees, alongside the river or near the facilities. I'll leave you to settle in and then, if you could let me know the site number, I'll enter it on my chart.'

'There's a shop?'

'I open between nine and twelve and then again in the evening between four and six. If there's anything you want urgently I can open in-between. I order milk and papers as necessary.'

'Sounds great.' Jack stood up. 'I'll go and get sorted out and then report back!' He grinned. 'Is the shop open now?'

'My daughter will be down in ten minutes to open up for you.'

'I need a few things so I'd appreciate that. But the village isn't far?'

'Larchpool is just over a mile.'

'I'll see you later.' Evie held out her hand and escorted her first customer back to his camper van. Watching him pull out of the yard and head off down the lane she turned, a smile on her face.

'What a pleasant man!' She smiled blandly at Owen who was glowering as he finished his drink before stomping out.

'Kate,' Evie called up the stairs, 'we've got our fist camper and he wants the shop.'

'Coming.' Kate bounded down the stairs, looking very attractive in cut-off trousers and a floating blouse. 'Is he tall, dark and handsome?'

'Well,' her mothered considered, 'he's certainly attractive. Too old for you though and remember, no flirting with the visitors!'

Jack Millington entered the shop a few minutes after Kate opened. He had parked by the river in the lea of an old oak and was smiling broadly.

'This really is an excellent location,' he enthused as he picked up a basket and scanned the shelves.

'I'm glad you like it.' Kate smiled politely and studied their first customer. 'You've picked one of my favourite spots. I'm Kate, by the way.' She held out her hand as he approached the counter.

'Glad to meet you.' Jack cast her an appraising look. 'Another charming member of the family. This is a new venture for you, I gather?'

Kate nodded. 'It's what the government calls diversifying!' She laughed. 'Mum and I think it's great fun. Dad has yet to be convinced.'

'He'll find it difficult,' Jack said shrewdly. 'All these strangers traipsing over his land.'

'It's only one field and we've plenty more pasture. We don't need so much now anyway.'

'Well, I hope it proves successful. I must say, I'm finding the whole set-up delightful.'

Kate waited until Jack left the site and then sped back to the farmhouse to relay the conversation to her mother.

'I wonder what he does for a living,' Evie mused. 'If he's travelling for a while, he must be well off. He certainly knows how to treat a woman!'

'Perhaps he's won the Lottery! You're right too,' Kate giggled. 'He's definitely rather dishy!'

'Kate!' Evie's face sobered and she shot Kate a warning look.

'There's no harm in looking.' Kate was still smiling. 'Perhaps a little old for me, but definitely my type.'

'Kate, that's enough!' Evie's voice was sharp and Kate suddenly realised her mother's gaze was reaching beyond her shoulder. She swung round and there, standing quietly in the doorway, his face impassive, was Grant.

'Oh!' Kate felt the colour suffuse her neck and face. 'I didn't hear you arrive.'

'The door was open.' His voice was cold. 'I didn't realise you were assessing the virtues of your guest.'

He threw a look of contempt at Kate and then addressed himself to Evie. 'I came to check everything was all right?'

'Fine,' Evie said. 'Mr Millington has settled in and been to the shop.'

'So I gather,' Grant said dryly. 'May I suggest you start on the records, Kate?'

'Of course,' Kate said stiffly. 'I'll do it now.'

She collected her mother's notes and flounced out of the kitchen. Setting off in the direction of Holly Cottage she felt annoyed and groaned inwardly. What a stupid thing to happen. She was only joking and now Grant must think her a complete airhead! That was the last time she would discuss their visitors unless she was sure her words would remain private.

'Blast,' she muttered. For some reason it rankled that Grant should have a poor opinion of her and she wished she'd been a bit more circum-spect.

She had almost finished filling in the spreadsheets when Grant walked in.

'Coffee?' His voice was cool.

'Thanks,' Kate replied meekly, feeling her face flush again.

The silence was broken by the click of her keyboard as he brewed two mugs of coffee and placed one on her desk.

'Everything in order?' he asked politely.

'Yes, thank you.' She leaned back in her chair and stared at him over her mug.

'I'm sorry you overheard my conver-sation in the kitchen . . . '

'It's no business of mine who you fancy,' Grant interrupted.

'I don't fancy Mr Millington!' Kate said, exasperated. 'I was only teasing Mum. If you must know, I think a bit of jealousy on Dad's part could be a good thing. It might make him realise Mum is still young and attractive and perhaps he should be a bit more attentive.'

'Your father knows how attractive his wife is,' Grant said quietly. 'He's not daft, you know. He's noticed her new clothes and the way she's enjoying the changes. He's worried that's all, and scared! I think making him jealous could do more harm than good.' His tone was reproving and Kate felt uncomfortable.

'Don't forget I've been here for weeks,' Grant said, perching on the side of her desk. 'I've had to instigate all the changes, talk it through with your father. He's feeling very insecure at the moment. His whole life has been turned upside down and he's not in control any more. Whereas your mother is enjoying every moment, she and Rosa find the whole scheme exciting. Your father feels alone and vulnerable. What he needs is reassurance, not more conflict.'

Kate sighed. 'I'm sorry,' she mumbled. 'I wasn't thinking.'

'Well, perhaps you should think a bit more before you take out your wooden spoon and start stirring again!' he admonished and Kate sipped her coffee, feeling like a schoolgirl caught out of bounds.

'Don't worry.' Grant was watching her face and smiled suddenly. 'It's all been a shock to you too. Once you've had time to assess the situation properly I'm sure you'll be an asset.'

Kate glanced at him sharply. He sounded rather patronising but Grant was smiling blandly at her.

'It would help Dad if he could make up this silly quarrel with George,' she said reflectively. 'I don't suppose you know what it was all about?'

Grant shook his head. 'It all happened before I arrived. Something to do with the meeting in the village hall and a difference of opinion, I gather, but no-one, including your mother, seems to know the exact nature of their disagreement. But it was obviously very serious to ruin a lifetime's friendship.'

At that moment the phone on the

desk rang and Grant reached over to answer it.

'Hello . . . ? Yes, she's here . . . wait a moment.'

Grant's eyes had cooled again as he handed Kate the phone. 'Someone called Dan?'

'Dan?' She was startled. 'What does he want?'

Grant raised his eyebrows. 'I suggest you ask him,' he replied coldly and walked out of the cottage slamming the door behind him.

Kate's heart sank. 'Daniel, what do you want?' Her voice was wary. She listened for a moment. 'You may be sorry, but I'm not sure I want to forgive you . . . No, there's nothing to discuss . . . '

She sighed. 'When are you back in this country . . . ? I see . . . No, Daniel, I don't think that's a very good idea . . . '

She held the phone from her ear. It had gone dead and she replaced it on the cradle with a feeling of foreboding.

Gloomily she returned to the farm. There was no sign of Grant and the day passed without a return of his presence. Kate didn't know whether to be glad or sorry and, as she slipped beneath the duvet that night, her thoughts were uncomfortable.

The rest of the week passed without incident. Two tents spread in Winterwood Meadow and the shop maintained its regular opening hours. Evie and Kate were so busy they had little time for gossip and Kate was amazed when she realised it was Saturday.

'You are going to the dance, Mum?' Kate asked over a hurried breakfast.

'We most certainly are!' Evie shot a glance at her glum husband. 'I'm looking forward to it.'

'Great. I reckon we need to leave about half seven if we can all get ready in time. Cheer up, Dad, it'll do you good to let your hair down for once!'

Owen grunted and, swallowing his tea, headed for the door. Kate looked at her mother enquiringly.

'Don't worry,' Evie said. 'He'll be there.'

'Are Ruth and George going too?'

'They are,' Evie said firmly.

'This should be worth seeing!' Kate grinned. 'Perhaps the silly blighters will bury the hatchet at last.'

'I sincerely hope so.' Her mother sighed. 'It would make things a darn sight pleasanter.'

In the end it was a rush to assemble in their glad rags for the outing but they arrived at the village hall just before eight. There were quite a few people already there and Rosa made a beeline for Sam. George and Ruth were seated and Ruth beckoned them over. Evie sat by Ruth and the two men sat, without acknowledging each other, at either end.

Kate giggled. 'You look like a pair of grumpy bookends,' she laughed. 'For goodness' sake, speak to each other!'

Both men glared at her and she shrugged and turned away, surveying the rest of the crowd. She spotted Jack

Millington in a corner talking to a local Councillor and then her eyes fell on Grant, who had joined Rosa and Sam at the bar.

Kate sighed. At that moment, as if aware of her gaze, he turned and his eyes locked into hers. For a second his face was still and then he smiled and Kate couldn't help responding. At least Grant didn't seem to bear grudges, even if her father did!

The music started and Evie turned to Owen. 'Come on,' she tugged his arm, 'let's have a dance.'

'In a while,' Owen muttered and Evie sank back on the seat deflated.

'May I?' The gentle voice startled her and she looked up into the enquiring face of Jack. She hesitated and then, casting a resentful glance at her husband, she stood up.

'I'd be delighted,' she murmured and Jack whisked her into his arms and around the floor. Owen stared after them, his face full of alarm.

'Looks like you've got competition,'

Ruth teased. 'Better watch out, Owen. Come on, George.' She pulled her reluctant husband to his feet. 'You are going to dance.'

Owen sat looking woeful until Kate plopped on to the seat by him. 'Come on, Dad,' she said gently. 'Don't spoil Mum's evening. She deserves a bit of fun — get up and dance with her.'

Owen looked at his daughter shame-facedly. 'Aye, lass, I expect I should.'

'You should,' Kate replied. 'Otherwise Mum might decide to go home with Jack!'

'You don't think she would?'

'Of course I don't! But I do think you need to show her you still love her.'

As the music stopped and Evie walked back across the floor, Owen stood up. 'The next dance is mine.' And, taking Evie's arm, he guided her back on to the floor. Kate heaved a sigh of relief.

The evening passed pleasantly, even Owen and George were seen to mutter at one another as the night progressed.

Kate caught up with friends and local gossip. It was good to be back.

She was busy chatting to an old school friend when she felt a light touch on her arm.

'May I have this dance?'

She swung round and, before she could reply, she found herself in Grant's arms as the band played a waltz.

He held her close and she was aware of his masculine smell mixed with a subtle aftershave. Giving herself to the moment, she closed her eyes and let herself drift with the music. He was a good dancer and she followed his steps easily. As the music faded away she felt a pang of regret.

'Thank you.' Grant released her and she felt coldness envelop her body. Taking her arm he guided her back to her parents. Evie and Owen were standing.

'We're thinking of heading home, Kate.' Her mother looked at her anxiously. 'Your father's a bit tired and we've an early start in the morning. But I don't want to spoil your evening . . . '

'Don't worry, Evie.' Grant spoke smoothly, his hand firmly pinioning Kate's arm. 'I'll drive Kate home when the dance finishes.'

'Are you sure?' Evie looked relieved. 'It would be a help.'

'No problem.' Grant smiled. 'After all, I go right by the door.'

'Then we'll head out.' Evie turned and bade farewell to Ruth and George.

'Now just a minute,' Kate managed to get a word in at last. 'I'm not sure I want to stay any longer!'

'It's all arranged.' Grant grinned.

Kate glared at him as her parents left the hall. 'I'm quite capable of making my own arrangements,' she said angrily. 'I've been halfway round the world on my own, you know. I certainly don't need looking after at a village dance!'

'Fine.' Grant's eyes were cool as he fixed her with an assesing look. 'Who else is going your way? Or are you prepared to walk the mile in the dark?'

Kate knew she was beaten and glared at him in silence.

'Right,' she muttered. 'But next time I'd like to be consulted.'

'Then stop behaving like a spoilt child and let's enjoy the evening shall we?' Grant said mildly. 'Ah I see Rosa is back, I think I'll go and sneak a dance.'

And, before Kate could utter another word, he had sped across the floor and taken Rosa in his arms, leaving a bemused Sam standing at the bar.

6

As the last waltz was announced Grant crossed the floor and, pulling Kate to her feet, swept her on to the dance floor. She glanced up at him as his strong arms twirled her into a spin.

'I take it you've no objection?' he said softly against her ear.

She shook her head, any idea of confrontation drifting away. She liked dancing with him; she couldn't deny that, so why not just enjoy the moment? They'd be at loggerheads soon enough, no doubt!

Smiling, she allowed her body to nestle against his and followed as he led her expertly round the small dance floor.

She let out a sigh as the music drew to a close and he looked at her quizzically. 'You obviously enjoy dancing?'

'Love it,' she replied.

Taking her arm he guided her through the crowd heading for the door. They walked across the car park in silence. It was a balmy night and Kate gazed at the myriad of stars above her head. A waning moon glittered through the evening mist as she stepped into the seclusion of Grant's Rover.

'Nice car,' she commented, glancing at his silhouetted profile.

'I need something reliable,' he replied. 'I travel a lot.'

'You must,' she agreed. 'I gather your job can take you anywhere?'

'Mainly in the Borders, but sometimes it can be further afield. And I like to get home occasionally.'

'Where is home?' Kate was curious.

'Wales,' he said. 'I've a cottage tucked away in the hills. Isolated, but it suits me. I need somewhere I can hide away sometimes.'

'I'll bet!' Kate grinned. 'I imagine diversifying can become very stressful, for you and the participants.'

'As you've discovered,' he answered dryly.

'Who looks after your cottage when you're away?'

'I've a lovely housekeeper, not far away. She pops in to keep the place aired and cleaned. I let her know when I'm coming home and she stocks the larder.'

'Sounds ideal.' Obviously there was no Mrs Drummond, Kate thought. She was surprised. She would have expected a man like Grant to have a partner somewhere. Maybe travelling so much put a blight on relationships.

'Penny for them?' Grant's voice broke into her thoughts and she felt the colour flare in her cheeks. She was glad it was dark.

'I was just thinking it must be a lonely life, living like you do,' she said rather lamely.

'I get by,' he said quietly. 'There's always plenty of company and any other commitment would be a hindrance at the moment.'

'Oh.' That put her in her place!

They turned off down the lane and the Rover swept into the yard. The lights shone from the kitchen window. Grant walked round and opened the door, holding out his hand to help her from the low seat. As she stood, he pulled her slightly towards him and she held her breath as his gaze locked into hers.

'Thank you, Grant.'

There was a tenseness between them and Kate felt unable to move. His face was in shadow but she could hear the catch in his breath and, suddenly, he tightened his grip and his arm circled her waist. She felt the hardness of his chest as she gasped and then his lips came down on hers.

Her heart hammered and, when eventually he released her, she almost fell, but his arms steadied her and she felt his warm breath on her hair.

'I'll see you in.' His voice was husky and the pressure on her elbow guided her towards the back door. Taking a deep breath to steady the shaking that seemed to pervade her body, Kate walked unsteadily up the path.

She pushed the open door. 'Would you like a coffee, Grant?'

'Why not?' His eyes were twinkling in the sudden light and she laughed lightly. Pulling away from his steadying hand, she stepped into the kitchen.

Filling the kettle, she fetched mugs as Grant lounged at the table, watching her. Her hands were awkward and the spoon clattered. His kiss had unnerved her and she tried to appear calm.

The silence was broken by the sound of voices and Kate felt a stab of annoyance. The door was flung open amid laughter and Rosa and Sam spilled into the room.

'Oh!' Rosa stopped short and Sam peered over her shoulder.

'Hi, Rosa.' Kate smiled and reached for more mugs. 'I thought you came home earlier.

Rosa blushed again and glanced at Sam.

'We were talking,' Sam said, grinning as he joined Grant at the table. 'Ah, coffee, lovely.'

Kate laughed and the tension was broken. Suddenly, they heard footsteps on the stairs and the hall door swung open.

'Came to see what all the noise was about.' Owen stood on the threshold, his dressing-gown tied clumsily around him, his hair awry. His gaze took in the gathering around his table. Rosa looked scared and Sam had flushed crimson. Only Grant appeared unfazed and stood up.

'Coffee, Owen?'

Owen grunted and shook his head, glaring at Sam. 'No, thanks!'

Rosa stood up. 'Dad, for heaven's sake, stop this nonsense!' She sounded close to tears.

Her father turned his glare on her. 'What?'

'I'm fed up with your sulking. It's about time you and George stopped behaving like spoilt children!'

'Rosa . . . ' Kate put an arm around her shoulder. 'I think that's enough.'

'Nothing's enough until our fathers patch things up!' Rosa was tearful again. 'It's just not fair on Sam and I. Come on, Sam . . . '

She shrugged off Kate's arm and caught Sam's hand, heading towards the door.

'But . . . ' Sam hesitated, but Rosa tugged again.

'Come on, Sam.'

Reluctantly he followed her through the door, a look of apology on his face as he lifted his hand to the silent group in the kitchen. The door slammed.

Kate turned to her father. 'Well?' she said. 'You know she's right, Dad. We've had a lot on our plate recently and we're all a bit tired, but it would help if you and George could sort out your problems.'

'Sorry,' Owen muttered and dug his hands in his dressing-gown pockets. 'I hadn't realised . . . didn't think . . . '

'It's been a long evening,' Kate

sighed gently. 'Go to bed. But please, think about what Rosa said.'

'Sorry,' Owen murmured again and shuffled out of the kitchen.

'Well,' Grant let out a sigh. 'Well . . . '

A muffled sob escaped from Kate and Grant was by her side in an instant. He put his hands on her shoulders and stared into her flushed face.

'Are you all right?' His voice was gentle. 'Oh, Kate!' He pulled her close and enveloped her in his arms.

She leant against his chest feeling his strength and comfort and, just for a moment, she nestled there, feeling the tension slip from her mind. Pulling away slightly she gazed up into his eyes, eyes that held a tenderness that made her heart somersault.

Then, just as Grant bent his head towards her, there was a knock on the door. Kate let out a gasp of annoyance.

'Whatever's the matter now?' she asked tetchily.

Grant grimaced and reached for the door handle. Flinging it open he stared into the pool of light and frowned.

'Kate,' the voice reached over Grant, 'I know it's late, but I've only just arrived and I saw the lights were on . . . '

'What are you doing here?' Kate whispered as she reached Grant's side. She felt Grant stiffen at her words.

'Who's this?' Grant's voice was harsh.

'This is Daniel,' Kate replied weakly.

'Daniel?' Grant stared at her, his lips a thin line and his eyes glinting.

'Kate's boyfriend!' Daniel stepped into the kitchen and reached a hand towards Kate. 'Don't tell me she hasn't told you about me?' He laughed and caught Kate's arm.

'Naughty Kate.' He leaned to kiss her cheek and she squirmed away.

'I'll leave you to it.' Grant stared coldly at them both.

'Grant, don't go!'

The door slammed, but not before Kate saw the expression of contempt in his sparkling blue eyes.

'Sorry,' Daniel smirked. 'Did I

interrupt something?'

'What are you doing here?' Kate repeated wearily.

'I told you when I phoned I was on my way. You gave me your address, remember? You told me to look you up when I came back to this country.'

'That was before you disappeared with Susie!'

'Yes, well,' Daniel shifted uncomfortably, 'that was a mistake. It's you I really love, Kate. Susie made a play for me . . .'

'And you couldn't help responding,' Kate said sarcastically.

'Sorry!' Daniel looked at her mournfully. 'Please give me another chance?'

Kate sighed. 'I take it you're in your camper?'

Daniel nodded.

'Then go and park up on the site. I don't feel like talking to you now.'

Kate held open the door, her face grim. Reluctantly, Daniel walked out of the kitchen and Kate shut the door firmly.

Wearily climbing into bed her mind raced through the evening, reliving the good and bad moments.

What a catastrophe! Whatever was she to do now? She realised that any feelings she had for Daniel had long since disappeared.

Surprisingly, she slept and it was her mother who shook her awake with a cup of tea. 'Wake up, sleepy head. There's work to do.'

Startled, Kate saw the time. 'Mum, I'm sorry. I've overslept!'

'You have rather,' her mother replied wryly. 'Don't worry, I think Rosa must have gone down to open the shop. When you've had your breakfast you can take over from her.'

Hurriedly dressing, Kate devoured a piece of toast.

'Mum,' she hesitated.

'Yes?'

'Last night . . . we had a new arrival. Someone I met in Portugal. He said he'd look me up when he got back.'

'It must have been very late?' Evie was watching her daughter thoughtfully.

'He's only staying the one night.' Kate said.

'Won't you want time to catch up?'

Kate shook her head. 'Not particularly. I'll have a chat obviously. But then he'll be moving on.' Kate hoped her confident statement was true.

'I see.' Evie carried on with the washing up.

Kate gulped the last of her tea and kissed her mum on the cheek. 'I'll go and relieve Rosa, and get Daniel to pay for his site.'

Evie watched as Kate set off down the track. She wondered what had happened last night, her daughter hadn't looked too happy about the situation, and where had Grant been in all this?

Her thoughts were interrupted as Owen came in for a drink. Making fresh tea she placed a mug in front of him.

'Good night, last night?' she asked casually.

'Mmm.' Owen was staring into space. 'I thought I might pop up to Hillside and take a look at George's new bull.'

Evie nearly dropped the plate she was wiping. 'Today?'

'Yes. I've nothing much on this morning.' Owen left without another word and Evie stared after him. So the dance had proved the turning point after all. It looked as if the quarrel between the two friends was about to be cleared up. She shook her head, smiling. It had turned out to be quite a night!

Down on the site Kate frowned as she reached the shop. The *Closed* sign was still on the door. She peered through the glass. There was no sign of Rosa. Running back to the farm she arrived in the kitchen, breathless.

'Rosa's not in the shop,' she told her mother.

'Not in the shop?' Evie echoed. 'Then, where is she?'

Feeling suddenly afraid they both mounted the stairs and entered Rosa's bedroom. The bed was made and there was no sign of Rosa.

'Rosa did come back last night?' Kate

said, feeling suddenly sick.

'What do you mean?' Evie asked sharply.

Kate recounted the scene with Owen.

'And she hadn't come in when you went to bed?'

Kate shook her head. 'I didn't think . . . What with Daniel turning up and one thing and another . . . I left the door unlocked. I never thought . . . '

'That explains that!'

'What?'

'The door was still unlocked when I came down this morning. Oh, no! She hasn't been home all night.'

'Mum, I didn't know! But she'll be with Sam. Ring Hillside, now.'

'Your father's just gone up there,' Evie muttered.

'He has?'

'To make his peace, I gather. So that's what triggered his sudden decision.' She was dialling Hillside's number.

'Ruth? . . . Is Sam with you, and Rosa? . . . What do you mean?' She glanced across at Kate, her expression serious. 'Owen's up with you? Then can you go and find them both and come down here. Quickly — we need to talk!'

She put the phone down slowly.

'What is it, Mum?' Kate sat down, her heart full of apprehension. 'What's happened?'

'They've run away, that's what!' Evie sank into a chair. 'Oh, dear heaven, what do we do now?'

At that moment the door opened and Grant put his head round the door. He glanced coolly at Kate and then addressed her mother. 'The shop's not open, I wondered where you were.'

'Oh, Grant, could you possibly cope with it for me?' Evie's voice was tearful as she fetched the key. 'I would appreciate it if you could, we desperately need help.'

'Why, what's happened?' Grant's face was immediately concerned.

'It's Sam and Rosa.' Kate's voice wobbled. 'After storming out last night, they didn't come back. They've run away!'

7

At Hillside, George had heard the Land-rover pull up and came from the barn.

'Owen,' he said gruffly. 'Good to see you.' The two men shook hands guardedly.

'Come into the barn, I'm just checking the tractor. I've got trouble with the starter.'

Owen sat on a bale of hay and stared at George as he fiddled with switches. Finally George looked up.

'Well, Owen?'

'We've been very selfish.' Owen shifted uncomfortably. 'I didn't realise until last night . . . I think we'd better make our peace George, for the families' sake,' he added hastily.

'Hmph! Maybe you're right.' George gave a wrench with a spanner. 'Lot of hot air about nothing, I daresay.'

'We were all worried. Maybe I said too much. This campsite's a worrying business.'

George snorted. 'Well, best not start on that argument again! Don't agree with what you've done, but there it is.'

There was silence for a few minutes and then the tractor burst into life. 'Fixed it,' said George with a grin. 'There's life in the old codger yet!'

'I thought I'd take a look at your bull.' Owen heaved a sigh of relief and stared at the subsiding tractor. 'Are you still putting him in the water meadow?'

Owen nodded. 'Best place for him,' he muttered.

'What about the right of way?'

'I've fenced him by the river.' George was tightening nuts. 'As long as your tourists don't stray from the path, they'll be no problem.'

Owen nodded. 'How are things, George?'

George shrugged. 'My Hereford bull should bring in a bit; expensive animal, but I reckon he'll be a good investment.

More farmers are turning to beef cattle, coming out of milking. They'll want good stock. I've replaced the sheep, Sam loved his sheep and, of course, Ruth's got a part-time job in the bakery.'

'I'd heard.'

'We'll get by.'

'The site's opened.'

'So I saw. Busy?'

'Some folks coming in. It'll get busier.'

George sighed. 'I'm sorry, Owen, but there was another good reason for me being so against it . . . '

'Besides tourists traipsing across your fields?'

'You know my sister, Doris, married Jim? They've got a farm on the coast.'

Owen nodded.

'Well, they've had problems. Came to the same conclusion as you — diversify. Met this company, going to help them finance a site on the field by the sea, going to make their fortune . . . and so on.'

'Well?'

'Well, finances got out of hand, plans became way above their funds, so the company offered to lend them money at a reasonable interest rate. They asked me about it — seemed a good enough deal at the time.' He shook his head gloomily.

'Should have advised them to see a solicitor, but solicitors cost money . . . ' He paused. 'I feel a bit responsible now,' he added gruffly.

'Why? What's happened?'

'Well, first the interest rates started to go up and Jim had a job to make repayments. Like you, he's just opened his site, but it'll take a while to build up business. Now the lending firm's getting difficult — want a lump sum back; even talking of calling in the loan.'

'Can they do that?'

'I don't know. Doris was on the phone this morning, all upset, asking for advice and I can't think what to do.'

'Oh, George, I am sorry — what a mess!'

'Would have mentioned it before, need some help on this, but . . . '

Owen sighed and patted his old friend on the shoulder.

'Don't take on now, George. We'll sort something out between us. You tell Doris to hang fire for a few days, fob the blighters off, and we'll have a think.'

'Thanks, Owen. I would be grateful. What with one thing and another, it's been a burden!'

'Aye, well,' Owen cleared his throat, 'a problem shared . . . '

'You didn't borrow money?'

'Not yet.' Owen shook his head. 'Managed so far on our few savings. Been waiting for the foot and mouth compensation. Things are tight, but we haven't had to borrow yet.'

'Thank goodness for that! Whatever happens, don't.'

'There's been no mention of it from Grant. But he works for government, so I doubt they'd be keen to let me have any money!' Owen chuckled wryly.

'Your Doris borrowed from a private company?'

George nodded.

'What's their name?'

'Let's think.' George rubbed his chin thoughtfully, 'it was all letters. Started with a G, GD something. Anyway, you steer clear of them. Now, let's go and look at this bull. He's a beauty!'

At that moment the door to the barn burst open and Ruth dashed in. 'Thank goodness I've found you both! Come on, we're going down to Stony Ridge.'

Owen was on his feet. 'What's the matter?' he asked in alarm. 'What's happened?'

'It's Sam and Rosa . . . they've run away.'

'Run away?' The two men echoed in unison. Ruth nodded. 'Quickly. Let's go.'

They were sitting at the kitchen table. The discussion had gone fruitlessly round in circles and Evie was feeling desperate. 'Should we call the police?' she whispered.

'I'm not sure,' Kate replied. 'Where on earth would they have gone?'

The ringing of the telephone disturbed their anguish. Owen was the first to reach it as they all dashed across the kitchen.

'Yes? . . . Doris? . . . '

'Doris?' Kate whispered.

'My sister?' George looked surprised.

Owen was talking quietly and then, 'Thank God!' He turned and smiled. 'We've found them!' He put the phone down and Evie burst into tears.

'They're safe?'

'Safe and well, but rather sorry for themselves.'

'What happened?' asked Ruth, also wiping tears from her cheeks.

'Apparently,' Owen said, 'they left here and spent the night in the car!' He grimaced. 'I bet that wasn't much fun! Then, this morning, they didn't know where to go, they hardly had any money on them and no change of clothes, so Sam suggested they went to Aunty Doris' and Uncle Jim's farm and, of course, as soon as Doris heard their story and realised we didn't know, she rang us. Thank goodness! Doris said she'd give them a meal and send them home. It's not that far. They'll be home by evening.'

'Right,' Evie said briskly. 'Let's get on. We'll deal with the children when they get home. I've some soup warming on the stove. I, for one, suddenly feel hungry!' They all nodded in agreement.

'And then we can get back to normal life!' She shook her head.

'Whatever Grant thinks of us all, I dread to think.' She glanced at the clock. 'He'll have shut the shop by now but we ought to tell him that they're safe.'

'I'll pop down to Holly Cottage if you like,' Kate ventured. 'It won't take me a minute.'

Grant was relieved to hear her news but, to Kate's disappointment, he remained cool and aloof and, after the traumas of the morning, she felt disinclined to explain about Daniel. She returned to the farm in a despondent mood.

Sam and Rosa arrived back at the farm mid-afternoon. They were shame-faced and apologetic. Much as Evie felt she should, she couldn't be angry with them and sent Rosa to have a bath and change her clothes.

Early next morning, Kate and Rosa were rearranging the shelves in the shop, Rosa staring critically at the final display.

'That certainly looks more attractive,' she commented and grinned. 'We need to make a profit on the shop if nothing else!'

Suddenly she hugged Kate and there were tears in her eyes.

'I'm sorry about . . . well, you know . . . ' Her escapade hadn't been mentioned again but Rosa still felt extremely uncomfortable about her foolhardiness.

'No harm done,' Kate said lightly. 'But don't you ever put us through that again, Rosa!' She punched her sister on the arm. 'Now, do you want a break or shall I go and do the paperwork?'

'I'll be fine here. It's all quiet at the moment . . . '

The door opened and Kate groaned. 'Hello, Daniel.'

Rosa looked enquiringly at the newcomer who was viewing her appraisingly.

Kate sighed. 'Rosa, this is Daniel. We met in Portugal.'

'Oh!' Rosa returned his stare.

'Let's take a walk,' Kate said determinedly and, catching his arm, she led him out of the shop. Rosa stared after her, bemused.

'Well?' Kate said as they wandered round the field. 'What do you want to say?'

'I've said I'm sorry, Kate. I know I hurt you; it was stupid.'

'OK, Daniel. I forgive you. You did me a good turn actually.'

'I did?'

Kate nodded. 'I've realised that our fling was just that, a fling; nothing more serious. I'm sorry you came all this way, but I really don't want to see you again.'

'I see.' They walked in silence for a minute and then Kate turned. 'I must go back to the farm. I've work to do. I take it you'll come and settle up and move on?'

Daniel shook his head. 'I'm not giving up that easily, Kate,' he said quietly. 'I expected you to be angry, but what we had was good. I have no intention of leaving here just yet. Besides,' he looked around, 'this is a lovely site. I want to spend a few days exploring.'

'You, exploring?' Kate said angrily. 'I've never known you be interested in the country! Please, Daniel, I'm asking again, please go away.'

They were back at the gate and she winced as he caught her arm in a vice-like grip.

'I mean it, Kate, I'm staying.' His voice was softly menacing.

Kate looked at him helplessly. 'You do what you want,' she said finally. 'But

119

don't include me in your plans.' She struggled to free her arm, his fingers bruising her flesh.

'Let me go, Daniel or I'll scream!'

'Trouble?' A soft voice interrupted. Kate hadn't heard Grant approach and she turned swiftly. Daniel's hand fell to his side.

'Just clearing up a few things,' Kate said.

'Sure you're all right?' Grant persisted.

'Daniel was just going,' Kate said, staring pointedly at Daniel. 'Weren't you?'

Daniel shrugged. 'See you around,' he replied and sauntered off across the field.

'Trouble in the love nest?' Grant's voice was sarcastic and Kate flushed.

'He's not my boyfriend.'

'Have you told him that?'

'I have actually,' Kate replied coolly. 'We knew each other, but that's all.'

'He hurt you badly, I take it?' They were walking back to Holly Cottage and

Kate scuffed her shoe against a stone.

'He went off with a friend, not that it's any of your business,' she retorted.

The matter wasn't raised again and the next hour passed swiftly. Over a hurried coffee at the farm mid-morning Kate heard about Owen's visit to Hillside.

'I'm glad you two have come to your senses at last, Dad,' she said and Evie nodded agreement.

'Yes, well . . . ' Owen looked rather shamefaced. 'I realised at the dance what a pair of idiots we were. And you were all suffering because of our stubbornness, so I thought I'd make the first move and then of course after yesterday . . . '

'Sorry, Dad,' Rosa mumbled.

'I can see his point about the camping,' Owen said reflectively. 'I didn't realise Doris and Jim were in trouble with their site.'

'Trouble?' asked Evie.

'Some firm loaned them money to start their venture, now they're trying to call in the loan and Jim can't repay it!'

'Poor Jim,' Evie said. 'I am sorry.'

'What company was it?' Kate asked curiously.

'Some development company. George couldn't remember the name. All letters, he said, began with G something or other.'

'GDP?' Kate asked, suddenly alert. 'Would that be the name?'

'Could be,' replied Owen. 'You'll have to ask George.'

As she finished her coffee her mind was spinning. Surely it couldn't be the same firm that Grant was involved with, could it? She determined to take another look at the folder when she got a chance. Also, it was imperative that she check out the agreement that her father had signed with the Small Business Initiative.

'I must get back to the office,' she said. 'I've some paperwork to finish off.'

'And I'm going into Larchpool,' Evie said.

'I'm going to inspect the fencing in the far field,' Owen contributed. 'Want to make sure the stock are secure.'

The family dispersed and Owen headed down the lane. Out of curiosity he walked towards the site. He hadn't taken much interest in the proceedings up until now, but he supposed he ought to make an effort. He opened the gate and entered the shop. Rosa looked up in surprise.

'Hello, Dad. I'm just ordering fresh supplies.'

Owen looked around. 'It all looks very attractive,' he said grudgingly.

The door pinged. 'Are you open?' Jack's voice cut in. 'Only I'm completely out of milk and gasping for a coffee!'

'Of course.' Rosa smiled. 'You're welcome. Help yourself.'

Jack picked up his milk and put change on the counter.

'Good dance on Saturday.' He smiled at Owen.

Owen grunted and eyed him warily.

He had been most uncomfortable about Evie dancing with their good-looking visitor. He hadn't felt jealous in years and it hadn't been a pleasant experience!

'Enjoy your coffee,' Rosa said as she handed him his change.

'I shall.' Jack grinned. 'I need to fortify myself before I walk into Larchpool.'

'You're going into Larchpool?' Owen queried.

Jack nodded and raised his hand. 'See you.' And then he had gone.

'What's the matter, Dad?' Rosa asked seeing her father's frown.

'Nothing,' Owen replied and left her staring after him as he skirted the site and headed through the woods.

'Nothing,' he muttered to himself, but an uneasy thought in his mind nagged at him. Evie was going into Larchpool, as was Jack, who had danced with her!

He felt ashamed of his thoughts. It was just his life was so topsy-turvy at the moment. He felt so unsettled, so unsure of himself. Anything could happen! Sighing, he tried to concentrate on the state of his fences and banish his fears. It wasn't easy.

8

At Holly Cottage, Kate opened the cupboard and reached for the file of agreements. Studying the papers and small print, she eventually closed the folder with a sigh. Everything looked in order. The Small Business Initiative was overseeing the project in the shape of Grant; funding was on a grant basis only. There was no mention of any permanent arrangement. She could find nothing suspicious. There was still no sign of Grant so she went to the drawer in his desk.

It was locked as she expected. She was so lost in thought she didn't hear his soft tread.

'Looking for something?' He entered the room and closed the door behind him.

'The file on GDP Ltd.' She caught her breath as anger flashed in his eyes.

'Now why would you want that?' he asked softly.

'I want to know what's in it!'

'Why?' he repeated. 'It has nothing to do with Stony Ridge.'

'It hasn't?'

He shook his head. 'It's another project I'm working on, miles away.'

'Financing land for development?' She saw him stiffen and his eyes narrowed.

'What do you know about GDP?' he asked quietly.

She shrugged. 'Not a lot.'

He watched her consideringly for a moment. 'Then I suggest you keep your nose out of affairs that don't concern you.'

Kate flushed at his tone. 'OK,' she said nonchalantly. 'It was just that the company has been mentioned in relation to . . . a friend, and having seen the folder on your desk, I wondered . . . '

'What friend?' He was still watching her, his eyes assessing, and Kate wished she'd curbed her anger and kept her knowledge to herself.

At that moment there was a knock on the door. Kate heard Grant mutter a curse under his breath as he flung the door wide.

'Yes?' he barked and then his lips thinned and he stepped back.

Kate could see the black Mercedes parked almost on the doorstep and she gasped. There was heavy breathing as the large man walked into the room and then stopped as he saw Kate.

'Sorry,' his eyes swept over her, 'I didn't know you had company.'

'This is an office, we're working,' Grant said brusquely. 'You should have let me know you were coming.'

'Something's cropped up . . . It was urgent . . . ' The man was still eyeing Kate speculatively. 'I came straight away.'

'So I see!' Grant's voice was harsh and his face grim as he turned to Kate. 'Can we continue our discussion later?'

'Of course,' Kate said smoothly,

recovering her wits. 'I'll leave you to your urgent business.'

'Aren't you going to introduce us?' The visitor's smile was wide.

'This is Kate, daughter of the farmer on whose land you're standing.' There was warning in Grant's tone. 'And this is . . .'

'No need to tell me.' Kate walked towards the door. 'Harry Gooding, nice to have met you.'

And, before the two startled men could respond, Kate walked out, closing the door gently. She grimaced as she crossed the yard.

'One up to me, I think,' she murmured. But at the back of her mind anxiety gnawed. What had Harry Gooding of GDP been doing at Holly Cottage and would she ever find out now she had no doubt alienated Grant?

In the cottage Harry was staring at Grant, who was looking baffled and angry.

'Well, Grant, I think we need to talk.' Harry Gooding plonked down at the table, a frown on his brow. 'How much does she know?'

'I didn't think she knew anything,' Grant said, exasperated. 'How the devil she knows who you are is beyond me!'

'You must have told her something,' Harry persisted.

'She saw the GDP file briefly, but it's been under lock and key ever since. She certainly didn't get a chance to open it.'

'Well, she recognised me from somewhere.'

'She mentioned a friend who had been involved with GDP . . . are you involved with anyone round here Harry? I sincerely hope you haven't been pulling any of your scams on friends of the Bramwells?'

'As if I would!' Harry replied smoothly.

'You would,' Grant muttered. 'Anyway, I wish you'd stay away from here, Harry; especially now. I don't want you coming here again.'

'Do we have a deal?' Harry rose and

pulled on his gloves.

'No we don't,' Grant retorted. 'I've told you before, Harry. Get out of my life!'

Harry's eyes narrowed. 'I can see you're not in a negotiating mood at this minute,' he said quietly. 'But remember — I hold all the cards. I'll give you time to calm down and reconsider. Then I'll be back.'

Grant groaned. 'Don't come back. If you must, phone me, but please don't come back.'

Kate had questioned her mother about Jim and Doris' financial problems, but Evie knew no more than the information Owen had imparted earlier.

Making a decision, Kate set off for Hillside. There was no way she could work in the office, and better to get the facts from George before causing any upset. Her parents had enough to contend with without her suspicions instigating greater stress.

At Stony Ridge Evie consulted her shopping list and set off for Larchpool.

She placed orders for papers and milk and then popped into the bakery to have a quick word with Ruth.

'Any chance of a coffee?' she asked.

'Find a seat.' Ruth indicated the small cafe at the far end of the shop. 'I'll rustle up a latte for you.' She smiled and Evie found an empty table in the corner where she checked her list.

'One latte.' Ruth appeared at her side. 'I'm afraid I can't join you, we're pretty busy today. See you later? About one-thirty for a snack?'

Evie hesitated and then grinned. 'Why not,' she said. 'I've a few more calls to make, so a bite to eat would be good. I'd like to have a chat.'

The queue was building up as Ruth slipped back behind the counter. Evie sipped her coffee and studied her list.

'Mind if I join you?' The soft voice made her jump and she looked up into the questioning eyes of Jack Millington.

'Not at all, please do.' Evie cleared the table and Jack put his cup down and sank into the chair.

'Nice village,' he commented as he took a long drink. 'Plenty going on.'

Evie nodded. 'Enjoying your holiday?' she asked.

'Very much.' He smiled.

Evie eyed him speculatively. 'What do you do, Jack? Or is that an impertinent question?'

Jack laughed. 'Actually, I'm a solicitor.' Jack stirred his coffee.

'Are you married?'

Jack hesitated and then smiled ruefully. 'There is someone actually,' he confided. 'Her name's Laura, but I've neglected her recently. The company I worked for closed and what with the upheaval and deciding my future — I took her for granted and forgot to share my worries with her. She thought I was losing interest, we had an almighty row, and I'm afraid I ran away.' He grimaced and Evie smiled sympathetically. She understood that feeling!

'It was the last straw really. I felt totally bereft; no job, no girlfriend, no future . . . So I bought a camper van, took to the road and the rest, as they say, is history.'

'Does Laura know where you are?'

Jack nodded. 'I've sent her a postcard from each site, hoping . . . you know.'

'You've told her you miss her?' Evie persisted.

'I've said I'm sorry, 'wish you were here,' that sort of thing.' Jack shrugged.

'Perhaps she'll be in touch, when she's had time to calm down,' Evie said, trying to console him. He was such a lovely man and she hated to see anyone unhappy.

'Don't worry. I've had enough of city life and besides, these days, most rural dwellers are in need of legal advice.'

'Perhaps you could do the occasional case on your travels?'

'Do you know of one?' Jack looked at her intently.

Evie hesitated. She wasn't sure if she should mention what she had in mind at this point, not before she talked to Ruth, but there was no harm in sounding out Jack's knowledge, was there?

'Well,' she hesitated, 'this is off the record at the moment, strictly between ourselves. A relation,' Evie continued, 'diversified with a campsite, just like us, only they borrowed money from a private company. The interest charged was good at first, then the company upped it and now it looks as if they might call in the loan. The family really need help.'

'Hmm.' Jack was looking thoughtful. 'Unfortunately, these loan sharks are pretty ruthless. Usually act just within the law too. But I'd be prepared to look at their contract if you wish.'

'Really?' Evie said eagerly.

'I'd need to know all the facts,' Jack said. 'If they'd be prepared to meet and show me the paperwork?'

'Would you?'

Jack chuckled. 'I'm afraid I would! I thought being a free man would be wonderful, and it is,' he added hastily. 'But I miss using the old brain cells and this sounds quite interesting.' He shouldered his rucksack and with a wave to Evie, left the café.

Evie could see Ruth was agog with curiosity, but the queue was still forming and with a quick, 'See you later,' Evie left Ruth in suspense.

Kate returned from her visit to Hillside in a thoughtful mood. Nibbling a biscuit, she leaned against the back doorframe and stared across the yard. George was convinced Jim was being swindled and was angry about the whole situation. To Kate's eyes GDP were indeed guilty of underhand practice and she wondered at Grant's involvement with the deal.

There was no doubt in her mind that Grant was somehow implicated in GDP although for the life of her she couldn't imagine him defrauding anyone. He had been so helpful with the diversification at Stony Ridge and nowhere could she find anything in the paperwork that said the deal was anything but above board.

So what had happened with Jim and Doris's project? She knew she had to get to the bottom of the riddle for her own peace of mind. Grant was continuously in her thoughts and she didn't want to be hurt again by another double-dealer!

'Speaking of whom . . . ' Kate muttered, as she saw the gate swing open.

'Pardon?' Daniel was smiling as he stopped in front of her.

'Nothing,' Kate retorted. 'You still here, Daniel?'

'I said I would be. Been for a walk round the farm,' he added as Kate stared at him stonily. 'Good acreage you've got here, the site should be profitable too. All be yours one day, I expect?' Daniel was watching her, his eyes calculating.

Kate looked startled. 'I haven't thought about it! You're gold-digging again, Dan. As I recall, you've never really worked in your life and how old are you? Twenty-five? You left me for

Suzanne because you found out her father owned a retail business, and now you think I'm a soft passage to a life of leisure. Think again, Daniel, I'm through with you.'

'Oh, come on, Kate.' His voice was rough. 'Just because I made one mistake . . . '

'What was the mistake?' Kate rounded on him angrily. 'Did her retail business turn out to be a corner shop?' Her voice was sarcastic.

Daniel walked towards her. 'Kate, please . . . ' He caught her shoulder and she twisted away, kicking his shin.

'If you touch me again . . . ' Kate threatened through gritted teeth.

Daniel laughed; a cruel sound and his eyes were sharp with venom.

'Oh, come on, Kate!' He lunged, and then spun round . . .

'I think Kate's made her feelings perfectly clear.' The voice was authoritative and Kate let out a gasp of relief as Grant stepped into the kitchen.

'I suggest you settle your debts and

move out.' Grant's voice was icy.

'Just going.' Daniel strode past Grant, shooting Kate a vicious look. 'For now. But I'll be back!'

The door closed and Kate sank on to a chair. 'Thanks, Grant, again.' Her smile wobbled slightly.

'I take it you'd like me to evict that young man?'

'Please, if you would.'

Grant grinned. 'I've always wanted to be a bouncer!'

Kate smiled weakly. 'Sorry for the nuisance.'

'Yes, well . . . ' Grant was watching her thoughtfully. 'You do seem to have caused a few problems since you've been home.'

Kate was on her feet immediately and Grant put up a restraining hand. 'Okay, okay!' He pretended to fend her off. 'I can see you're slightly touchy at the minute. I'll go and deal with Daniel and then I think we should talk.' His eyes had narrowed. 'In the office, at three o'clock?'

Kate nodded and let out a breath as he left the kitchen. Hopefully Grant would sort out the problem of Daniel, but that still left Harry Gooding. Cutting herself a sandwich she stared out of the window, George's words echoing in her mind.

In the cafe Ruth leaned across the table towards Evie. 'So, spill,' she whispered. 'Tell me all about the assignation.'

'It wasn't an assignation!' Evie laughed.

'Well, you looked as if you were having a deep discussion.'

'Ruth, will you stop jumping to conclusions. You'll be giving the gossips a field day and then what would Owen say!'

'Might shake him up a bit, make him jealous.'

'I don't want to make him jealous,' Evie said gently.

'Anyway, what was your meeting all about?'

'Let's get one thing straight, Jack

came in purely by chance and happened to sit at my table . . . '

'And . . . '

'We got talking.' Evie leaned back in her seat, grinning annoyingly.

'Evie, if you don't spill the beans I'll go and tell the whole village you had a clandestine meeting with one of your tourists.'

'Clandestine, in the village café? Come on, Ruth.' Evie giggled. 'Oh, all right.' She took pity on her friend and recounted the conversation with Jack.

'Well I never!' Ruth looked bemused. 'Fancy that.'

'Do you think Jim and Doris would talk to him?'

'I don't see why not.' Evie looked thoughtful. 'I'll have a word with George. I know he was trying to get them to take some action, but Jim was a bit wary of legal bods, after everything.'

'I'll ask him about it.'

The two friends parted and Evie drove back to Stony Ridge in thoughtful mood. Kate was still in the kitchen and mother and daughter pooled their knowledge on the GDP affair. Kate's heart sank even lower but she kept her knowledge of Grant's involvement to herself.

'Anyway,' Evie straightened up, 'I must get on, otherwise there'll be no dinner tonight!'

'Well,' Kate laughed, 'if you will have dates with the tourists, what do you expect?'

'Dates with a tourist?' Owen's voice was full of alarm as he entered and pulled off his boots. 'What's been going on?'

'I'll leave you to it.' Kate winked and left.

'Well, Evie, what did she mean?' Owen's voice was anxious.

Evie blushed. 'Oh, Owen!' She kissed the top of his head. 'I haven't had a date with a tourist. Jack Millington happened to come in while I was having coffee and he sat at my table. In full view of all the customers I might add! We had a very interesting conversation . . . '

'I don't want to hear,' Owen said brusquely, noticing his wife's heightened colour.

'But Owen . . . ' Evie turned from the sink, astonished. 'Honestly, you will want to hear this, don't be so silly . . . '

'I'm not being silly . . . Owen muttered and, before Evie could utter another word, he stomped up the stairs.

9

Evie sighed exasperatedly. Really, Owen was so touchy lately. Just when the problem of his quarrel with George was solved and she thought things were getting back to normal, he had to take umbrage because she had coffee with Jack. She would never understand men! Surely, after all these years, Owen didn't think she would be seriously interested in another man, did he? She shook her head. Honestly!

As she turned into the yard at Holly Cottage, Kate's steps slowed. She wasn't looking forward to this meeting. The door opened at her first knock and she followed a stern looking Grant into the kitchen.

'Sit down, Kate.' Grant indicated a chair and she sat meekly.

'Now,' he placed himself opposite, 'I suggest you tell me how you know

Harry Gooding.'

'I looked him up on the Internet.' The words rushed out and a look of surprise passed across Grant's face.

'The Internet?'

She nodded. 'I saw the GDP file on your desk and when you locked it away I became suspicious. My parents are very trusting and I was afraid there was something underhand going on,' she finished lamely. Grant was watching her.

She shifted under his scrutiny. 'I thought I'd better check out the company. It's a development company.' She looked at him accusingly.

'And you immediately jumped to the conclusion that GDP was involved with the site on Winterwood?'

'It seemed likely.'

'Really?' Grant's eyes were thoughtful as he digested her words. 'And why would a development company be interested in a campsite?'

'I noticed they've built some larger leisure sites in several areas.'

'And you think it's likely they'd want to do the same in Larchpool?' His smile was quizzical.

She shrugged. 'It was just a thought,' she muttered.

'And do you still think there's some underlying plot by GDP to develop Winterwood?' he asked at last.

Kate shrugged. 'I've been through all the documents for Stony Ridge,' she admitted.

'And you can't find any mention of GDP,' Grant finished for her.

Kate shook her head.

'That's because,' Grant continued, 'Winterwood is a totally different project. It has no connection with GDP at all.'

'So why is the GDP file here, in this office?'

Grant sighed. 'I'm a freelance consultant, Kate. At Stony Ridge I'm working for the Small Business Initiative; elsewhere I'm working on other projects. This happens to be my base at the moment, so all my current projects are being co-ordinated from Holly Cottage, and I need the paperwork to do that!' He smiled slightly although his eyes were anxious.

Kate had to admit his explanation was plausible. 'So,' she said slowly, 'are you involved in another project that is using GPD?'

'Would you have an objection to that?' His eyes narrowed.

'I would actually . . . '

A hammering on the door cut off her words. Grant uttered an exclamation and rose, flinging the door open. Jack stood there looking extremely dishevelled.

'Come quickly,' he panted. 'One of the tourists is trapped by a bull.'

Jack stepped into the kitchen looking harassed. 'Explain,' Grant demanded as he reached for his boots.

'I walked back from Larchpool over the hills, and then followed the footpath through the meadows to the wood, which brings you back to Winterwood.' Jack's breath was calming. 'When I got to the meadow I saw the bull on the far side by the river.'

'And?' Kate prompted as he took a breath.

'Then I saw this lad come out of the wood. He seemed to undo the fence . . . I shouted, but he didn't hear me. Then the bull started towards him. Saw freedom I suppose . . . '

Grant reached for a stick.

'Anyway, before I could get across the meadow, the bull had somehow got round the fellow and he was in the corner, between the river and the wood and the bull was pawing the ground and snorting, just looking at him.

'By the time I raced across the chap was yelling. I told him to stay quiet and I would get help. But it's a long way through the wood to your cottage. I dread to think what's happened in the meantime.' Jack looked upset.

'You've done all you could,' Grant said. 'There was no way you could take on a bull by yourself. Whatever was the stupid idiot doing?'

'Heaven only knows!' Jack shrugged.

'You go on.' Kate had picked up the phone. 'I'll ring George at Hillside, it's his bull. I'll see if I can get hold of Dad as well.'

Grant and Jack left and Kate explained the situation to Ruth and her mother, then she rushed after Grant.

It seemed a long way across the site and through the wood but eventually they ran into the meadow. Kate drew a sharp breath as she took in the scene. Perched precariously on a fallen tree trunk that jutted out into the river, was Daniel, looking terrified. On the river bank the bull was grazing lazily.

Kate started to giggle and, as Grant glanced at her, a grin spread across his face. Jack looked bewildered.

'What's going on?' he demanded.

'It couldn't happen to a nicer person,' Kate murmured. 'You say you saw Daniel break the fence, Jack?'

Jack nodded.

'Then it serves him right,' Grant agreed. 'Perhaps we should leave him there?' He turned, and there was an anguished howl from the river.

'Help me, please,' Daniel cried. 'Get him away!'

'I understand you let him out?' Grant shouted.

'I didn't mean to!' Daniel wailed.

'I think you were out to cause trouble, Dan,' Kate said.

Daniel shook his head miserably.

'If we remove your attacker will you promise to leave the site, immediately?' Grant's voice was hard.

Daniel nodded.

At that moment George came tearing across the field in the Land-Rover. Leaping from the vehicle he came across and examined the fence.

'It's been forced,' he said in disgust. 'See this bit here? Where the wires are twisted? Someone's gone to a lot of trouble to undo that!' He took a pair of pliers from his pocket and started to wind the strands together.

'That someone is stranded on your old tree,' Kate said.

'Yes, well, he can wait. Bull's most important. At least he hasn't got out. I'll make him safe and then we'll see about rescuing the culprit.' He turned as Owen arrived on the scene.

'I could sue you know!' George glared at his friend who groaned.

'Oh, please, George, let's not fall out again. There's no harm done and we'll make sure the culprit is punished.'

'Hmph!' George tested the fence. 'That looks strong enough now.' He glanced across at Daniel and grinned. 'I should say the blighter has probably learned his lesson anyway.'

'Hey,' Daniel's voice was full of alarm as George headed back to the Land-Rover, 'isn't anyone going to help me?'

Grant looked at Owen. 'What do you think?'

'Well,' Owen rubbed his chin thoughtfully, 'I suppose we'd better think of something. Don't want a dead tourist on our hands!'

There was a yell from the river as the bull moved closer, oblivious to the concern he was causing.

'You'll have to get in the river,' Owen shouted. 'It's shallow there. Walk along the shingle to the end of the field.'

With that Owen turned away and winked at Grant. 'He's going to be wet, but it might make him think before he tries that stunt again!'

They walked back across the field, Kate giggling slightly as Daniel splashed and grumbled his way through the water. Climbing out through the trees he shook himself like a dog and glared at the smiling group.

'Don't know what's so funny!' he snarled.

'I suggest you get back to your camper and get dry,' Grant said coldly. 'You're lucky the bull wasn't hurt and there was no damage. Otherwise you'd have found yourself with a hefty bill.'

Daniel cast him a baleful look and glared at Kate.

'Go and pack up, Daniel,' she said quietly. 'Get off Winterwood before

George changes his mind and decides to report you.'

Daniel turned and stumbled away. As they entered the site they saw his camper van lumbering up the track.

'He hasn't had time to change his clothes,' Kate exclaimed.

'Has he paid?' Grant looked at her and she shook her head. 'I'm afraid not. But I think that's one bad debt we'll write off, with thanks.'

It wasn't until they'd made a pot of tea and filled Evie in on the details of the escapade that Kate remembered her unfinished conversation with Grant. By then the evening was drawing in and she felt extremely tired. Any more discussions would have to wait until the next day.

As she was preparing for bed the telephone rang. She heard her mother answer it and then Evie appeared in her doorway.

'Well,' she seemed pleased, 'that was Ruth. She's spoken to Jim and Doris and they'd like to have a chat with Jack about their loan. They're coming over to Hillside tomorrow.'

'Good heavens, that's quick. Will Jack be around?'

'I'll pop down and see him first thing in the morning.'

'I wouldn't mind being there when they have the meeting,' Kate said thoughtfully. 'I've an interest in GDP.'

'And Grant's involvement,' she thought.

She wondered if there'd be time to talk to him before the meeting the next day. It was rather essential in the circumstances.

She slept soundly, the excitements of the day exhausting her and, awaking early to a radiant sun, she grabbed a quick breakfast and headed for Holly Cottage. As she left the yard she heard her mother call and, turning back, saw her leaning out of an upstairs window.

'Kate I need to talk to you . . . '

'Shan't be long.' Kate blew a kiss.

Evie sighed in exasperation and shut the window. 'Why couldn't she have waited a minute?' she muttered. 'I could have saved her the journey!'

The cottage door was locked. Taking the key from its hiding place Kate let herself in. The kitchen looked unusually tidy and there was no sign of Grant. Annoyed, Kate headed back to the farm. In the kitchen Evie heard her daughter stomp in and turned.

'I tried to catch you,' she said.

'Why, what's happened?' Kate was suddenly alert. 'Where's Grant?'

'That's what I was trying to tell you,' her mother said. 'If only you hadn't been in such a rush.'

'Tell me, tell me what?' Kate demanded, alarmed.

'It's Grant,' Evie said gently. 'He's gone.'

10

What do you mean, Grant's gone?' Kate echoed. 'Gone where?' Her heart was hammering.

'He had some problem to sort out at home,' Evie explained. 'He called here very early this morning — I'd only just got up — said he needed to go urgently. Something about family problems . . .'

'Family? What family?'

Evie shrugged. 'I don't know. He's never said much about his personal life. Anyway, he won't be around for a few days and, as everything's running smoothly on the site now, we'll cope easily.'

'I suppose so.' Kate was still stunned by the news. 'You don't know when he's coming back?' she persisted.

'He didn't know. He said he'd ring us. I've got his phone number if you need to speak to him urgently?'

Kate shook her head. 'It doesn't matter,' she mumbled.

'We've got to get used to him not being around anyway,' Evie continued. 'His work here is practically finished, so he'll be moving out soon. You can have Holly Cottage back,' she finished brightly.

'Mmm.'

'What's the matter, Kate?' she asked gently.

'Nothing.' Kate roused herself. 'Nothing at all.' How could she admit her feelings for Grant to her mother? 'Have you spoken to Jack?' She forced a smile.

Evie nodded. 'The meeting's all set up for four o'clock.'

'Good. I'll be there. In the meantime, I'd better go and do some work.'

At the farmhouse Owen had come in and picked up the post. He let out a whoop that made Evie jump. She spun round.

'What on earth . . . ?'

'It's the compensation cheque! It's finally come.' He hugged Evie and

157

waltzed her round the kitchen.

'Wonderful!' She hugged him back. 'That's marvellous news. At long last! I expect George will have had his, too. Well, we shall see this afternoon.'

'This afternoon?'

'Yes.' Evie spoke determinedly. 'I need to talk to you, Owen, and now you're in a good mood it seems the right time. Sit down,' she ordered.

Owen sat, a look of alarm on his face.

'It's all right, it's nothing terrible,' Evie said gently. 'It's about Jack.'

'Oh, Jack!' Owen's shoulders slumped.

'For heaven's sake, Owen, you don't really think I could fancy another man, do you?' Evie said irritably. 'Surely you trust me more than that?'

'Of course I trust you!' Owen retaliated. 'But things have been so bad I thought . . . '

'That I'd leave a sinking farm? Have you forgotten our vows: for better for worse?'

'It's certainly been worse lately,' Owen said gloomily.

'But I love you, Owen, and Stony Ridge. I'd never leave you, whatever.'

Owen looked mortified. 'Sorry, my dear. I'm not myself lately.'

'I know.' Evie placed a hand across his as they sat together at the table. 'Now, will you let me tell you about Jack and why I've been talking to him?'

Owen nodded shamefacedly.

Evie explained the situation and Owen perked up when he heard about the meeting that afternoon.

It was a large group that sat round the kitchen table at Hillside. All eyes were focused on Jack as he perused the documents Jim had brought and analysed the information he had been given.

'The paperwork seems in order,' he said at last, looking up grimly. 'Companies like this prey on the ordinary man, lull him into a false sense of security, lend him money and then bump the interest rates up.'

'I was afraid of that,' Jim sighed gloomily. 'I had a feeling we'd been done. Well, I can't repay this month's amount, it's far too high, so they'll just have to wait until we get more business, or the compensation cheque comes in. It looks as if that might come soon as you've had yours.'

'There's something else,' Jack said hesitantly.

'What?' Doris looked alarmed.

'The small print, here.' Jack held up the last sheet and Jim squinted at the tiny letters.

'Can't read that,' he grunted.

Jack sighed. 'I'm afraid it says that if you go into debt with them for more than one month they have a right to ask for full payment of the loan and, if that's not forthcoming, they can then claim the land.'

'Take the land?' Jim bellowed. 'They can't do that!'

'I'm afraid they can.' Jack passed the papers back. 'It looks as if they've got you over a barrel. How late are you with your repayments?'

'Just one month,' Jim answered gruffly.

'The interest has almost doubled and it's due by the end of the month. After that . . . Well,' he shrugged, 'we're done for.'

'So you've got a couple of weeks to raise the money. Have you tried the bank?'

'Tried them in the first place. Wouldn't help. Don't know where to turn.'

They all stared mournfully at one another.

'I'm so sorry,' Jack said. 'If I could help . . . '

'Well, at least we know the worst now,' Jim said. 'I didn't know they could take the land, so we've got to do something. I was just going to carry on and hope they'd be lenient. By the look of it, they were after my land all the time.'

'They're a development company,' Kate said. 'I think they own a chain of commercial caravan sites. They seem to specialise in developing land that has good profit potential. If farmers need to borrow to diversify, there's kindly old Harry Gooding with his beaming smile, making it easy for them. He advertises himself as 'a philanthropic firm, using waste land for community use'!' She explained how she had looked GDP up on the Internet.

'I bet they get all their land this way,' Jack said grimly. 'They're on hand to dole out the money, just when it's needed and then, wallop, they've caught their fish, hook, line and sinker! The farmer can't make the repayments, they claim the land, get planning permission, develop the site and make a fortune.'

'What are we going to do?' Doris asked.

'I don't know yet.' Jim stood up. 'But I'm not giving up without a fight.'

'Good for you,' Jack applauded. 'I'm just sorry I can't be of more use.'

'You've helped a great deal,' Jim said grimly. 'I would have lost it all if you hadn't read the small print. Now I'm going to fight.'

Kate was very quiet on the way back to Stony Ridge.

'Mum,' she hesitated and then plunged on, 'do you have Grant's address?'

'Of course.' Evie sounded surprised. 'Why?'

'Because I need to see him,' said Kate in a rush. 'If GDP are going to repossess Jim's land, then I need to know what involvement Grant has with the company. It's only fair to tell him . . . '

'I agree,' Evie said gently. 'You're right, Kate. Grant's been very good to us. We couldn't have managed without him. As I understand, it's only just over an hour's drive from here. Sunnybank is the name of the house, just outside Rhayader, in Wales. I've got the full address somewhere . . . ' She rummaged in her desk. 'Why don't you set off in the morning? Nothing's going to happen before then and it'll give you all day to get there and back.'

'Will he be there?'

'I imagine so, but you could always ring him.'

'Perhaps I will,' Kate agreed. 'But in the morning. Otherwise he might decide to go out for the day.'

'Is that likely?'

Kate sighed. 'I don't know,' she said. 'I really don't know what Grant might do.'

Early next morning Kate dialled Grant's number. 'Yes?' His voice was terse.

'Grant, I need to talk to you urgently. I'm coming to see you.'

'I'll be here.' He hardly sounded welcoming but Kate smiled grimly and put the phone down. She had studied the map and was pretty sure of the route.

Evie watched her go, consternation in her eyes. She had a shrewd idea how her daughter felt about Grant, but how Grant could be involved with Doris and Jim's problems, she couldn't imagine. She realised when Kate returned from Portugal that someone had hurt her badly and, when Daniel appeared on the scene, she guessed he was the cause of Kate's pain. She'd been thankful when that particular problem had left the site!

Now, though, she wondered whether Kate was going to be hurt again. She had taken a liking to Grant and he had been an absolute boon during the last few weeks, but she knew so little about him . . .

She was so lost in thought that she didn't hear the knock until it was repeated strongly. She opened the door to see a smartly dressed lady, an anxious look on her face.

'Can I help you?'

The woman hesitated and then smiled doubtfully.

'I hope so.' She looked at Evie for a moment and then plunged on, 'I'm looking for Jack Millington, he said he was camping on your site?'

Her face suffused with colour and Evie smiled in delight.

'Are you Laura?'

The visitor looked startled, but nodded.

'Wonderful!' Evie exclaimed. 'He'll be so pleased to see you. Go down there,' she came into the yard and pointed down the lane, 'his camper van's parked by the river, under a tree. You can't miss it!'

She beamed at the surprised Laura who, muttering a quick thanks, set off to the site, a bemused look on her face.

Kate found Sunnybank easily. Asking in the nearby village she was given directions and set off under the curious gaze of the locals. She wondered if Grant had many visitors, very few if the surprise shown in the shop was anything to go by.

The small stone house nestled in the lea of towering rocks, gorse and wild flowers strewn on the patches of coarse grass. Sheep grazed peacefully and Kate could see buzzards gliding gracefully in the morning sunshine.

There was no answer to her somewhat timid knock on the front door so she followed the path round the side of the house and then stopped dead in her tracks. The path opened into a yard surrounded by a low stone wall and there, parked by the back door, was the black Mercedes.

Kate took a deep breath and marched angrily to the door. This time her rap was answered almost immediately and Grant stood there, a look of consternation on his face. 'Kate, you're earlier than I expected.'

'I told you I was on my way.'

'Yes, but I thought you'd ring for directions.'

'You thought wrong!' Kate retorted. 'Can I come in?'

'Of course.' Grant held the door open.

She followed him into the kitchen where Harry Gooding sat glowering.

'Harry was just leaving,' said Grant pointedly.

'Was I?' answered Harry.

'Harry, don't you think it's about time you saw sense?' Grant's voice softened as he put a restraining hand on the older man's arm.

'I saw sense?' Harry blustered and stared from one to another.

Kate stepped back. She didn't understand what was going on between the two men but she could feel their tension as they both stood, motionless, waiting.

'Please, Harry, stop this now; stop this vendetta. Nothing can bring Martha back.'

'How dare you mention her name!' Harry's voice was dangerously quiet.

'I dare, because I know she would hate what you're doing; ruining ordinary folks' lives, preying on the vulnerable, wasting all your expertise on petty revenge, and none of the families deserve your anger, none of them are responsible for Martha's death.'

'If you'd stayed loyal . . . ' Harry's voice cracked.

'I can't stay loyal to someone who destroys others. I backed you up as long as I could, Harry. I owed you that much

. . . But now — Martha would've hated what you've become.'

There was silence as Harry slumped beneath Grant's hold. He rubbed his hand across his eyes and shook his head.

'I gotta go,' he mumbled and turned towards the door.

He stopped in front of Kate and looked at her pleadingly. 'See if you can talk some sense into my son!'

Kate stepped back, her expression bewildered.

Grant?' Kate said tentatively.

'I'm sorry, Kate, you shouldn't have been a witness to such a scene. I'm so sorry . . . '

'Do you want to tell me what that was all about?' There was silence as Grant filled the kettle, the sudden harsh flush of water seeming deafening. 'What did Harry mean, when he called you his son?'

Grant sighed as he made tea and placed a steaming mug in front of her. 'It's a long story, Kate.'

'Is he really your father?'

'Sort of. Are you going to tell me what was so urgent?' He ignored her question.

Kate shook her head. 'I'm not telling you anything until you explain,' she said. 'What I need to discuss involves Harry Gooding and GDP.' She glared at him and he smiled ruefully.

'OK,' he agreed finally. 'I'd better come clean.'

Kate grunted and sipped her drink, watching the man opposite her.

'The story goes back a long way,' Grant began at last and hesitated. 'My mother died when I was born,' Grant started uncomfortably, staring into his mug. 'My father . . . ? I don't know. Anyway, I was adopted by an older couple, plenty of money, unable to have children. I had a good childhood.' His voice was sad.

'My adoptive mother died a few years ago and my father went to pieces. Anyway he rallied, he had his own business and, when that started to slide, he pulled himself together and rescued his firm. But he'd changed . . . '

'How?' Kate was digesting what Grant said and gradually piecing together the information he was disclosing.

'He became hard, ruthless, he started doing business deals that, although they weren't illegal, were definitely shoddy. I'd gone into the family business when I left school,' Grant added. 'I was supposed to take over one day, it seemed a good future, but people were getting hurt, ordinary folk with very little money were doing deals that left them bankrupt. They'd trusted Harry.'

'Jim and Doris,' Kate breathed and Grant looked at her sharply.

'I started to disagree with Harry and finally pulled out of the firm. As you can imagine, he was none too pleased!' Grant grimaced. 'I didn't do anything about his misdealing; I owed him something after all, but my loyalties became more and more divided.

'I went freelance and worked for the

Small Business Initiative, setting up various diversifying projects. I got back my self-respect. I hadn't heard from Harry for a couple of years, so I could push GDP from my mind. Cowardly I know . . . '

'But understandable in the circumstances,' Kate murmured.

'Anyway,' Grant continued, 'Harry found out about my farming diversifications and tried to muscle in, pulling the old loyalty strings and so on. He threatened to expose the deals that I had been involved with in the past, get me sacked.'

'But he would have ruined GDP.'

'I don't think he cares any more. Although he did back off when I called his bluff and told him to go ahead. We'll see, he might just do that.'

'Were you involved with the deal with Jim and Doris Speedwell, George's sister and her husband?'

Grant shook his head. 'That was after I left. Is that what you've come to see me about?'

Kate nodded and filled him in on the details of the meeting with Jack. 'I needed to know what your involvement was, before it went any further.' She looked at him anxiously.

'I assure you I wasn't involved with that one.' He touched her hand across the table. 'But thank you for coming.' His eyes held hers for a long moment and Kate felt her heart begin to race.

'I had to,' she said shakily.

'I'm sorry I haven't been honest with you.' His fingers were caressing the palm of her hand. 'I've been trying so desperately to put the past behind me and I was sure you'd hate me if you knew the truth.'

'I don't hate you.' Kate's arm was tingling. 'Far from it!'

'Oh, Kate!'

Suddenly Grant was on his feet and pulled her into his arms. 'I've tried so hard not to love you,' he murmured into her hair. 'I intended to clear out of Holly Cottage and let you get on with your life. I saw what losing someone you love did to Harry, and inadvertently to me; I was determined never to allow myself the luxury of falling in love.'

'You can't be held responsible for Harry's mistakes,' Kate murmured.

'But surely I could have done something?' His eyes were agonised, as he looked down at her.

'You did, you left. And besides, Harry wasn't doing anything illegal so there really was little you could do.'

'True.' Grant sighed. 'All the same, it's been eating away at me.'

'You should have told someone,' Kate said gently.

'I had no-one to tell! Until now.' His arms tightened around her and she breathed deeply against his chest.

He reached down and his finger lifted her chin. Turning her face to his, he stared into her eyes for a long moment before his lips claimed hers.

At last he released her. They were both shaken and Grant ran his fingers through his hair.

'So, where do we go from here? I'm afraid I've fallen in love with you, Kate.'

Kate couldn't stop grinning as she caught his arm and they sat side by side.

'I love you too, Grant,' she whispered. 'So now you don't have to worry alone any more. I'll stand by you whatever you decide to do about Harry.'

'Thanks.' His eyes glowed. 'I don't think there is much to be done at the moment. But we can do something about Jim and Doris, and maybe, in time, Harry'll see the error of his ways. He was such a good man, once.'

Kate picked up her tea and took a sip. 'Urgh, it's cold!'

'I'd better make a fresh cup. Then I'll take you to lunch at The Fox Inn in the village. They do a fair bar snack and we've so much to talk about.'

It was a happy couple that strolled into the quaint bar and, amid inquisitive looks from regulars, they settled in a corner seat and held hands as they sat together.

'This'll give the local gossips a field

day!' Grant grinned. 'Let's order, I'm starving.'

After an excellent meal they leaned back and stared at one another. 'Right,' Grant said. 'To business.'

'Jim and Doris.' Kate nodded.

Grant looked pensive for a moment. 'I think Jim might have a difficult fight on his hands. As I said, Harry was very careful to stay within the law.'

He thought for a moment. 'Do you know the full amount of the loan?'

Kate shook her head. 'Jim didn't actually mention a sum, but Jack would know.'

'Can you find out, when you go back?'

Kate looked surprised. 'Of course, if you want me to.' She looked at him for a moment as he stared into space.

'Why?' she asked suspiciously. 'What have you got in mind?'

'Let's just say I think I might be able to solve the problem and throw a spanner into Harry's little game!'

'Really?' Kate grinned. 'Are you sure?'

'Not until I know the amount. Don't raise their hopes too far, just say I'm working on a solution and not to do anything until they hear from me.'

'Grant, you're wonderful!' Kate flung her arms around him excitedly and there was a chuckle from the locals at the bar.

Flushing, she drew away and stood up. 'I think I'd better make tracks. Mum will be wondering what on earth's happened to me.'

They left the village and returned to Sunnybank, Kate collecting her car and saying a reluctant goodbye.

'You will come back tomorrow?' she asked anxiously.

'Try and stop me!' His arms tightened around her. 'We've a lot of plans to make, once we get Jim and Doris sorted, and a whole new future to think about.'

True to his word, after an early call from Kate, Grant returned late the following day. He bounded into the kitchen and grinned at Evie.

'Can you call a meeting tomorrow, with Jim and Doris?' he said.

Evie looked at him in amazement. 'Tomorrow?' she gasped.

'Afternoon,' Grant said firmly. 'I think I've solved their problems. Oh, and would you also ask Jack to come?'

'I'll ring Ruth now.'

The meeting was arranged and it was an excited group that sat in the kitchen at Stony Ridge the next day. Jack proudly introduced Laura and Evie gave her a hug.

'I'm so glad you two are back together,' she whispered and Laura smiled shyly as she settled in a chair close to Jack.

'Firstly,' George was beaming, 'can I tell you my good news?'

'Carry on.' Grant leaned back in his chair.

'My compensation cheque came yesterday!'

'Wonderful!' Owen beamed.

'It won't solve all the problems, of course,' Jim said soberly. 'But it will help.' He looked expectantly towards Grant.

Grant cleared his throat, 'I don't know if any of you know I have a history with Gooding Development Projects?'

He looked enquiringly at Kate who shook her head.

'Well,' he continued, 'suffice to say I have, so I know Harry Gooding well. There have been times when I should have spoken out and I didn't,' he said regretfully. 'But that's all water under the bridge now. This time is different, this time I can foil his plans and help out.'

They all looked at him agog. 'My adoptive mother was Harry's wife. She died some years ago.' There was silence in the room as they digested this information. 'When she died she left me a legacy, unbeknown to Harry, which I've invested and it's now a sizeable sum. I propose to lend some of it to Jim, interest free, to pay off GDP in full.'

There was a gasp.

'The money can be repaid as and when the business will allow. There's no hurry. I have no need of the capital at the moment.'

'I can't accept this,' Jim said gruffly.

'Whyever not?' Kate asked.

'Of course you can,' Doris interrupted firmly. 'Don't be so stupid, Jim. This is a chance to keep our land and make a go of the site.'

'But . . . ' Jim looked at her crossly.

'Swallow that stupid pride of yours!' Doris glared at him. 'Thank you, Grant, we'd be delighted to accept your offer.'

At that moment Jim's mobile phone rang and he escaped to the kitchen. A few minutes later he returned, a shocked expression on his face.

'That was Harry Gooding,' he croaked.

'What's he done now?' Grant said grimly.

'I don't believe it!' A grin was spreading inanely across Jim's face.

'Believe what?' Kate demanded.

'He's reduced the interest and he's deferred payment of the capital until the business is in profit!'

Grant dropped his head in his hands.

'You're sure?' Kate whispered.

Jim nodded, his expression dazed. 'He says he's had second thoughts . . . he doesn't want to deprive me of my business . . . he'll put it in writing . . . '

'Good heavens!' Owen exclaimed. 'How marvellous!'

The enormity of the telephone call sank in and suddenly there was a babble of excited talk.

'Are you all right?' Kate stroked Grant's hair and he raised his eyes to hers. She saw tears.

'I'm just fine,' he managed.

Owen hugged Doris in delight.

Jim looked shamefaced as he clapped Grant on the shoulder.

'It was very generous of you,' he said gruffly. 'I'm sorry about . . . '

Grant waved his hand. 'Forget it,' he said and smiled. 'I'm so glad Harry's had a change of heart. But if you ever need help, you know where to come.'

'Do you really think he's changed?' Kate asked and Grant shrugged.

'We can only hope,' he said quietly.

It was a happy party that shared tea and cakes before Jim and Doris set off home. George and Ruth departed too and Kate wandered down to Holly Cottage with Grant.

'I'm sorry I ever doubted you,' she said at last.

'It's understandable.' He squeezed her arm. 'I was pretty secretive about GDP. Afraid, I suppose. I've been afraid of a lot of things since I left Harry. Afraid of what he was doing, afraid to trust anyone because of this, afraid you would find out about my background and hate me.'

'Hate you?' Kate turned and stared into his eyes, eyes that looked as blue as a sun-kissed sea. 'How could I ever hate you, Grant? I love you.' And, standing on tiptoe, she pressed her lips to his.

When they finally separated, breathless, Kate was smiling. 'Perhaps now you two can patch things up, and I can get to know my future father-in-law properly!'

Grant looked down at her for a long moment and then crushed her to him.

'I'll call him tomorrow,' he whispered into her hair.

Jack and Laura, returning to camp-site, saw the lovers and smiled, slipping quickly away down the path to Winter-wood Meadow.

THE END

We do hope that you have enjoyed reading this large print book.

Did you know that all of our titles are available for purchase?

We publish a wide range of high quality large print books including:
Romances, Mysteries, Classics
General Fiction
Non Fiction and Westerns

Special interest titles available in large print are:
The Little Oxford Dictionary
Music Book, Song Book
Hymn Book, Service Book

Also available from us courtesy of Oxford University Press:
Young Readers' Dictionary
(large print edition)
Young Readers' Thesaurus
(large print edition)

For further information or a free brochure, please contact us at:
Ulverscroft Large Print Books Ltd.,
The Green, Bradgate Road, Anstey,
Leicester, LE7 7FU, England.
Tel: (00 44) **0116 236 4325**
Fax: (00 44) **0116 234 0205**

Other titles in the
Linford Romance Library:

FOLLOW YOUR HEART

Margaret Mounsdon

Marie Stanford's life is turned upside down when she is asked to house sit for her mysterious Aunt Angela, who has purchased a converted barn property in the Cotswolds. Nothing is as it seems . . . Who is the mysterious Jed Soames and why is he so interested in Maynard's? And can she trust Pierre Dubois, Aunt Angela's stepson? Until Marie can find the answers to these questions she dare not let herself follow her heart.

A LOVE WORTH WAITING FOR

Karen Abbott

In the lovely village of Manorbier in Pembrokeshire, Jasmine gets the opportunity to open up a teashop — her dream come true. However, disturbing events threaten her business prospects, forcing Jasmine to search her heart and discover who wants the teashop closed. Is it the controlling boyfriend she has put in the past? Or someone wanting the premises for himself . . . local artist Rhys Morgan, for instance? Jasmine has to put her heart on hold until the sinister campaign is over.